L.A. Blues II:
Slipping into Darkness

L.A. Blues II:
Slipping into Darkness

Maxine Thompson

www.urbanbooks.net

Urban Books, LLC
78 East Industry Court
Deer Park, NY 11729

ISBN 13: 978-1-60162-351-5
ISBN 10: 1-60162-351-8

First Trade Paperback Printing June 2012
Printed in the United States of America

10 9 8 7 6 5 4 3 2 1

Distributed by Kensington Publishing Corp.
Submit Wholesale Orders to:
Kensington Publishing Corp.
C/O Penguin Group (USA) Inc.
Attention: Order Processing
405 Murray Hill Parkway
East Rutherford, NJ 07073-2316
Phone: 1-800-526-0275
Fax: 1-800-227-9604

L.A. Blues II:
Slipping into Darkness

Maxine Thompson

Acknowledgments

2 Timothy 1, 2: 4. "But know this, that in the last days, critical times hard to deal with will be here. 2. For men will be lovers of themselves . . . lovers of money . . ."

I want to thank my Heavenly Father for helping me through this novel. I struggled with writing this novel, first, due to a broken leg and ankle, followed by subsequent water damage to my home. However, this turned out to be a fortuitous event, which had me living and writing from a hotel room, so that part worked out. But, sadly, at the end of the year, and the beginning of the next, two young lives were both tragically taken within my family.

As prophesied in the Bible, we are living in critical times, hard to deal with. The forty year war on drugs is just one element of the many negative things impacting our community, which I explore in *L.A. Blues II*.

I thank my readers who have embraced the series, LAPD-turned-Private-Eye character, Z. She still has a long journey in front of her. In this series, I hope to capture some of the times we now live in with this lingering recession hangover. I thank all the book clubs, including Suzetta Perkin's Sistah's book club, who have read *L.A. Blues* in January 2012. I understand the discussion was lively, which is a good thing. I don't write about pretty subjects, but I address the things we need to heal.

I thank Carol Mackey of Black Expressions, LaShaunda C. Hoffman, Editor, Sormag, Tamika Newhouse, AAMBC, Rawsistaz Book Club, Urban Reviews, and all the Black Book Clubs.

I thank the Urban Book Family. Publisher, Carl and Martha Weber, Natalie Weber, and the other staff for your part in the African American literary renaissance.

I thank the listeners to my Internet radio show on Artistfirst. I'm coming up on my tenth year hosting Internet radio shows to promote authors, publishing, and the written word.

I thank my network of writer family, mentor/friend/sister/ Dr. Rosie Milligan, Shelia Goss, Suzetta Perkins, Michelle McGriff, N'Tyse, Tracie Loveless-Hill, and friend, Pat G'Orge-Walker.

I'm still seeing too much loss of young life and potential talent in our community, and hope that the L.A. Blues series will help young people think about choices and consequences.

This book is dedicated to the memory of Debra Nicole Thompson (Sunrise: 6-5-90 to Sunset: 12-30-11) and Robert Jordan, III, (Sunrise: 7-27-89 to Sunset: 1-10-12.)

You can contact me at maxtho@aol.com.
You can find me on the web at:
http://www.maxinethompson.com
http://www.maxinethompsonbooks.com
On twitter at Safari61751
On Facebook as Maxine-Thompson
On Linked-In.

The world is a dangerous place; not because of the people who are evil; but because of the people who don't do anything about it.

—Albert Einstein

Chapter One

Hollywood Kodak Theater

We need your help, Zipporah I Love Saldano.
They say they will kill your brother if you don't get
that money.

> Your mother, Venita

"Oh, no," I groaned, putting my palm to my
forehead as I read my mother's text message on
my latest state-of-the-art iPhone. I was sitting
in a white stretch limo in front of the Hollywood
Kodak Theater with my man, Detective Romero
Gonzalez. I was surrounded by my foster sister,
Chica, her husband, Riley, my frenemy, Haviland, and her live-in boyfriend, Trevor. Our various perfumes were mingling and rivaling with
one another's, casting a heady mix of Egyptian
jasmine, iris, and gardenia throughout the limo.

Romero, arm draped around my shoulder,
was seated next to me. We were facing the
other two couples who sat across from us. He
reached out, gently touching my hand. "What's
the matter, *mamí?*"

I shook my head, too overcome to speak. I
hadn't told my lover about my latest dilemma.
I moved my hand away, grasping my phone.

"Go ahead," I urged Romero as I beckoned my head toward the door. The chauffer opened the door and Romero was the first to step out. "I'll catch up with you."

My hands trembled as I tried to type back an answer. I felt like the sun was burning my hand, as if I were sitting in the eye of the devil. This was serious when my moms—Venita, an OG who didn't play—was calling me by my middle name, I Love (which happened to be the same as hers). This was also another way of her playing her trump card: the mother's guilt card. Not that she had any right to play that card, but that's another long story. All I knew was she was pulling out all stops.

I typed back: What money? I can't help you. I'm sorry. "It's really crazy being the responsible one in the family," I hissed through my teeth, speaking to no one in particular as I shut off my phone, not wanting to hear my mother's next plea. I shook my head. What did my moms expect me to do—rob a bank to get the ransom money?

Anyhow, what money? I had no idea what she was talking about. Now, what in the sam Twinkie (yes, you heard me right; I don't cuss as part of my twelve-step program) did Venita expect me to do? I ain't God. I just solved a messy case with my nephew Trayvon's murder and was trying to get my bearings. As long as I worked with strangers, I could remain objective, and effectual. But when you worked with loved ones, it was hard to be detached. Your heart got in the way. Besides, when did I ever catch a break? I just want to live out my life in peace. I wanted a quiet life. Forget this mess.

I was dressed to the nines, trying to forget my problems, and getting ready to take pictures of my friends as they walked the red carpet. I just wanted to snap pictures and stay in the background. Was that too much to ask? I had a press pass and a professional Canon digital camera in tow. Besides that, I had a covert reason for being there. I was also looking for information on a missing starlet, Lolita, for a family member. They thought she might have been one of the victims of the black serial killer, the Grim Sleeper, but so far we hadn't found any trace of her. She'd been missing for over a year. She was last seen with actor Justin Howard, who'd been interrogated but released. As a hunch, I was just snooping around here. Kind of to kill two birds with one stone.

Earlier, we'd attended the balloon releasing ceremony for the mothers of murdered children, so this was ending the day on an upbeat moment. That was, up until I received a call earlier from Venita. Now she was sending this text since my ringer was off. Absently, I shook my head. No, I just couldn't get involved. No telling what Mayhem could be involved in. I wasn't getting killed fooling with him.

On top of everything else, I had a license as a private investigator to protect, and, although I didn't always walk the fine line of the law, I tried not to be shady. (One thing I must admit, though, is sometimes the line between good and evil did get a little smudged for me.)

"Who were you texting?" Chica asked.

"My moms."

Chica leaned in, a look of deep concern furrowed on her brow. "Any news on Mayhem?"

I shook my head. I hated the fact that my brother got caught slipping. *What happened to all his bodyguards?* I wondered. Especially his lieutenant, that big dude who looked like Michael Clarke Duncan. Where was he when this kidnapping went down?

"Are you sure you can't help?"

I didn't answer Chica. What could I say? My brother, Mayhem, the Crips kingpin, had been missing for a day so far, and I couldn't put off what I'd planned. After all, I had a life.

"Who was that?" My friend, Haviland, the fashionista of the three of us women, interrupted before we got ready to exit the limo.

"Venita."

"Well, what are you going to do? Why don't you go to the police?" Haviland gave me a probing look.

At any rate, I wished I hadn't even told her at the Mothers for Murdered Children March earlier that day what was going on, but she'd overheard me and Chica talking about it. "I can't go to the police." I shrugged my shoulders.

I bit my bottom lip to keep from cussing Haviland out and relapsing from my profanity-free Lent fast. I caught myself in time. Instead, I just glared at her as if she'd sprouted two heads. "Which part of my brother is a drug dealer don't you understand?"

"Well, excuse me for asking." Haviland sounded miffed.

Didn't she have any street smarts? I guessed not. Born of a black father and white mother, she was adopted at birth and raised in Beverly Hills with a white family, who, (unfortunately for her) since the father's death, had disinherited her.

Now, poor Haviland had to get her hustle on for the first time in life. No longer the trust fund baby, she had to get off her butt and grind like the rest of us. Truth be known, I didn't think she was doing everything legit now that she had to carry her own little dookie bag, either.

"Is there a problem?" Trevor, the white liberal, leaned in and whispered toward me as he was easing his way to the door.

"Mind your own beeswax," Haviland snapped. She really was mad at me, but was afraid to talk smack to me.

"Why are you always so cantankerous?" Trevor whined on his climb out of the limo.

"Eat shit and die," Haviland sniped, sounding like a white girl in a black girl's body. She stuck out her chin defiantly. "Don't start nothing with me today." She gave Trevor the finger as he stood outside the limo.

Trevor, who was a younger Brad Pitt look-alike and up-and-coming soap opera star, stood at attention outside the limo, posing on the red carpet. He acted as if nothing had happened. He was grinning a bright Colgate, capped-tooth smile.

"Why don't you go catch up with your boy-friend?" I shooed Haviland with my hands so I could step out the limo before the brawl was on. "I'm going to do my thing."

Just as quickly, Haviland slid back into her Hollywood façade, stuck out her hand daintily, and waited for the escort to help her out the car.

"I don't give a frizzuck about that little dick fool," Ms. Hollywood (as Chica and I called her behind her back) whispered under her breath as she stepped out the limo. She strutted a few steps as skittish as a young colt before she got ready to be escorted down the red carpet. She turned to the cameras, flashed a bright TV-commercial smile, then hooked her arm into Trevor's inner arm like they were Hollywood's happiest couple. I watched her sashay down the red carpet as if she owned the world.

Chica and I glanced at each other, then burst out laughing. We shook our heads at the same time. *No need to say it. Haviland is crazy.* Privately, I cringed inside. See, people like Haviland give black women a bad rap. She would cuss out her white boyfriend at the drop of a dime whenever we'd double date. Sometimes I wished Trevor would just call Haviland the B word, or the N word, and get it over with.

As far as I was concerned, Trevor was too politically correct. Haviland would cut up so bad, all in the name of "relationship transparency." I wished she'd go to the opposite extreme. Sometimes she just gave too much information. She told all of Trevor's shortcomings in the bedroom, when we were out in public as couples on double dates. Let's just say, maybe there was something to be said for fronting as a couple.

Because of the disrespectful way Haviland acted toward her man, Romero was always uncomfortable to be around them as a couple. He didn't like the way Haviland emasculated her man in front of people. A year ago this wouldn't have bothered me at all. I would have called Romero machismo and a male chauvinist. But, for the first time in my life, I had no problem letting a man wear the pants in the relationship.

Romero told me when we first started seriously dating, "I know you're a strong woman, Z, but both of us can't wear the pants in this relationship."

Ironically, this had never become a problem either. Romero kept me purring like a kitten. Yes, I had to admit it. I was whipped. Everyone said they'd never seen me act so submissive or content with a man. They all said Romero brought out my softer side. He also treated me like a queen.

Chica turned to me as the escort was getting ready to help us out the car. "*Mija,* you pimping that dress," she complimented me as Riley was climbing out.

"Thanks. You're banging the mess out of yours too," I said. "LYLAS," I mouthed to her (love you like a sister) when it was her turn to climb out of the limo.

"Me, too." Chica blew me a kiss.

Actually, we were closer than sisters. Although she was a Latina, she was family. Which made me think of my dilemma again. *Mayhem. Isn't he family too? What am I going to do?*

I forced my mind to think about my dress. I knew Chica was sincere with her compliment and that she was telling the truth about my dress. I looked hot in this dress, the way it clung to my curves. The back was out on the dress and I didn't have any washtub rolls on display, thanks to the tae kwon do I'd been taking. I blushed as I remembered how Romero had torn the dress off me and made passionate love to me before we left home. I guessed he would agree the dress was sexy too.

But a little voice inside of me kept beating me over the head with a stick. *How can you be at the Academy Awards when your brother has been kidnapped?* It wasn't like I cared who won the awards. As far as I was concerned, this was a big favoritism party anyway.

Well, one side of me wanted to help, but the other side of me was totally against it. I just couldn't get in trouble fooling with my crazy brother and his madness. Why should I stick my neck out? First of all, I had this night planned for months. Plus, I had two free tickets to the Academy Awards, so that we could get some PR for our upcoming reality show about our three businesses. I had signed on for a part in Haviland's reality show, which would surely bring me big fat paychecks from Hollywood stars needing a private eye. I'd already warned

Chica not to get into cat fights with us or we'd bounce in a heartbeat.

Our show would be called *Women in Business*. I would expose some of my duties as a private investigator, Chica's role as a bounty hunter, and Haviland, the lead actress, a former child star turned wedding planner, would show the world of Hollywood marriages. Recently, we had rented an office space together in Santa Monica where we planned to film, as well as at Haviland's Hollywood Hills mini mansion. We were even thinking of spinning off a business magazine by that same name for women in business.

So, as you see, I had too much to lose. I'd been sober for over two years. My new business, Saldano Private Investigations, was thriving. I had a good relationship with my man, Romero. I didn't need any extra stress or drama that might make me fall off the wagon.

"I feel guilty that I'm out having fun like this." Chica's words interrupted my reverie as I stood next to her, with Romero's arms around me. Riley was on Chica's other side, his arms embracing her.

I gazed at Chica's fawn-colored eyes, which were watering up, and noticed a sad look flit across her sienna-hued face. Her eyes took on a wounded look. Sorrow had etched premature lines in her young face. I knew she was thinking of her son, Trayvon, who was murdered a year ago at the age of fifteen. Without warning, my foster sister's grief could turn into an aggressive cancer, one which would return at any given moment.

I reached out and grasped her hand and squeezed it. For a moment, we each held each other's free hand. Almost as in a mirage, I could still see the same blood pact we'd made as girls. In fact, as adults, we'd both shed blood behind Trayvon's untimely death. Although my murders were public knowledge, Chica's murders were our unspoken secret. It also was part of our bond.

Letting her hand go, I changed the subject to try to cheer Chica up. "Hey, do you see Denzel?"

Just as quickly, Chica's mood shifted like an L.A. sun peeking out from under the clouds of an overcast gloomy June day. She pulled her hand out of Riley's hand. "Where?" She tilted her head to peer out of her eyes sideways. "Look! Will Smith and Jada are here too." She tried hard to contain her excitement. In an effort not to point, she lifted her eyebrows in their direction.

"There's Oprah, and look! Jennifer Hudson," Chica added under her breath. "Look at all that weight Jennifer's lost. She looks amazing!"

"Doesn't she?" I agreed, also speaking sotto voce.

Riley leaned in and hugged me. "Thanks for cheering her up, Z. I appreciate how you're helping her grow her business too."

I flagged my hand in dismissal. For a moment, star gazing had helped distract me from what was really bothering me, too. I was amazed at the chiseled faces, many which came compliments of the local Beverly Hills plastic surgeon.

Some faces were soft, improved for their efforts; some were macabre looking, almost like masks.

Without warning, that subterranean side of me reared its illogical head. Blood calling to blood. And blood won out every time. I felt a protective urge. Just the thought of anyone harming my brother hit me with a double punch of fear in my gut. I surely couldn't go up against some cartel or the Bloods or whoever was holding my brother. Sheesh! Who gave my brother up?

Chapter Two

We each stepped out the limousine to the setting sun and the blazing flashes of the cameras as were ushered into the world of the beautiful people—"Hollyweird" as they called them on the Black gossip blogs. The paparazzi, here en masse, resembled locusts descending on a lush garden. I couldn't help but feel the blaring contrast to my private world and the public celebrity world I was now about to enter. Now we were about to become reality stars. Well, at least Haviland was—Chica and I would have bit roles in her program. But it was all good because, in the big picture, we all would get customers for our businesses.

Romero looked spectacular in his Bond-like Savile Row tux and could have passed for a famous Hispanic actor himself. People said he resembled Academy Award winner Javier Bardem.

We each took our time strolling down the red carpet at the Oscars. Actually, I had a press pass; the others were all guests. Today I was looking "Hollywood" myself, clad in Haviland's borrowed black Versace dress. I was even wearing fake eyelashes. I'd been taking martial arts for protection, and now had a side benefit—this new fit, muscular body. Haviland had lost twenty pounds for the night, too, and she was down to almost a three, so she really could get away with the plunging neckline on her Kaufman Franco dress. Chica was rocking the mess out of an Oscar de la Renta gown, also compliments of Haviland.

Tonight, in addition to borrowed clothes, we were all living borrowed lives, which was pretty much what actors do all the time. We were all given invitations because of Haviland's boyfriend's nomination for his role in his first film, a suspense thriller, *The Red Herring*.

Before Romero and I strolled all the way down the aisle to our seats, I motioned for him to follow me. "I'm not going to be sitting with you, babe."

"I know. I just wanted to walk in on the best-looking woman's arm here tonight."

I grinned. "Thank you, boo. You're so sweet."

Without warning, Romero's phone vibrated and he looked down at his phone. Someone was sending him a text message.

"Is everything all right?" I asked.

He shook his head as he began to type an answer. "I'm all right. No, it's a case I'm working on. This is really important."

"Gotta go?" I gave him a sad puppy-dog gaze and pouched out my bottom lip in a cutesy pout.

He nodded, and brushed his lips against my forehead. "I'm sorry. I'll make this up to you." Then he leaned back, scrutinizing my face to see if I was mad.

"Promise?"

"When I get home, we'll pick up where we left off."

A tingling roared between my legs just at the thought of my Latin lover's sexual prowess. Goose bumps of excitement made my nipples harden. Since I was wearing a sheer, backless bra, self-consciously I slumped my shoulders in, trying to hide my arousal.

"You so bad." I blushed, trying to hide my grin.

Romero glanced down at my nipples through my dress. "No, you're the naughty one. Tiger!"

That was our inside joke. I lifted my eyebrows at him in the way that was usually our signal when we were ready to make love. Romero softly patted my waistline. Although I tried to act ladylike around him, he knew I was quite the tigress in the bedroom. I liked how Romero always made me feel feminine, which was kind of hard to feel in my line of work. I took the same risks as any soldier did.

"I'll take a rain check. Do what you gotta do, babe." I frisked my fingers in a "get gone" signal. "I know how it is." I was reminding him of my decade tenure on the streets as an LAPD officer, before I became a PI. And sometimes it got rough on the streets, even in my new profession.

"You're sure now?" Romero looked doubtful, as if he thought I would hold this against him.

"You know this isn't my thing either." I waved my hand in a flourish around the gala of Hollywood's celebrities and stars. Although I was looking forward to the after party, I was here partially on business, too. "I'm just here for this dog-and-pony show for Haviland. I guess it will add a little cachet to our show, too."

Romero looked relieved. "Thanks! You're the best." He pecked me on my lips. With that, he turned and left. Although he had to leave, I was glad he'd come.

I pulled out my press pass that Haviland had confiscated for me, and flashed it to the escort. That Haviland could get her hands on anything.

She was the youngest person I ever knew who went to her doctor and got a prescription for medical marijuana. Although she was in a Narcotics Anonymous twelve-step program for her OxyContin addiction, she was now claiming she had glaucoma. By the way, she was still paying a blackmailer who helped her stage a home invasion last year, which kept her from losing her mini mansion in Hollywood Hills. She was also no stranger to the bail bonds person, and managed to teeter, if anything, just this side of the law. I'm telling you. In spite of her innocent appearance, that girl was scandalous.

When I worked as a policewoman, I'd evaluate someone like Haviland as a sociopath, but since we met in a drug program two years ago, we'd become quasi-friends of sorts. She would do anything for me, but I just didn't trust her as far as I could see her.

After everyone was on the carpet, I excused myself. Although I was looking forward to the after party, I stepped over to the media section and began flashing pictures with my camera. I flashed pictures of various stars as they pro- filed and floor-showed. I flashed pictures of my friends as they milled around in the crowd before they were seated by the ushers.

In spite of my forced, fake smile, I was not a happy camper. Something kept tugging at me. I guessed it was my conscience. What was I go- ing to do about that crazy brother of mine?

I hated to have to be the one to break Venita's bubble, but I was not getting involved in May- hem's kidnapping. After the run-in I had last year with two dirty cops, I was already consid- ered suspect as a private eye. No one seemed to remember that these narcs had killed my part- ner, James Okamoto, shot me, then later killed my fifteen-year-old nephew, Trayvon, because they mistook him for me.

Even though I killed them both in self-de- fense, from that point on, I could tell I was under surveillance by the powers that be. Trust and believe, though, I didn't lose any sleep over those two murders, either. I felt it was kind of a street justice to them. An eye for an eye. Now and then, the Feds or the police would still pull me in and harass me.

With Romero gone, my mind meandered back to my brother's dilemma. As far as this kidnapping of my brother, Mayhem, I couldn't even go to the law with this anyhow. My brother was a Crip, a known drug dealer, and a lethal killer.

And why was my mother coming to me? As far as I was concerned, Mayhem had always been her pet. She was the one who did twenty years' time for a crime my brother, her first born, committed. Let her figure out how to get him from his kidnappers. I knew I was hardening my heart when I told this to myself.

Still, this thing wouldn't let me go. I was in a quandary. *Venita must be crazy.* I liked living. No telling who could be holding Mayhem, from some Mexican cartels to a Black gang. Because I felt so conflicted, it was hard to concentrate on my surroundings.

I forced my mind back on the present, and did what I came here to do. I started snapping pictures of celebrity couples who would probably be divorced and remarried by next year, since they didn't believe in letting any grass grow under their feet. If I were the paparazzi, I'd be sitting on a gold mine right now, since I was capturing all the A-list actors and actresses, but at the same time, I was looking for a lead on my case. Lolita, the missing person, was last seen with a D-list actor, who so far I hadn't seen tonight.

Romero hadn't been gone twenty minutes when, out of my peripheral vision, I noticed a couple of suits approaching me with the intensity of two fence-jumping alligators. I knew the look. I guessed they were Feds of some kind.

"Come with us, young lady."

"Why? I didn't do anything wrong? What the—"

Chapter Three

"Wait a minute. I got rights," I protested.

"You got the right to be arrested right here. Don't make a scene." The taller man with the glass eye spoke with a threatening rumble under his voice. A spasm of irritation crossed his face, and his good eye narrowed in contempt.

A strong hand grabbed me by the elbow. It was Glass Eye's partner.

"Wait a minute. Who are you? Wha . . . Who . . . ?" I stammered.

"FBI. Special Agent Jerry Stamper." He flashed a badge, then stuck it back in his jacket before I could eyeball it good. His crew cut had dandruff snowflakes powdering his navy serge jacket.

Glass Eye flashed his badge. "Special Agent Richard Braggs, DEA."

"Oh, is this some kind of cluster fuck? Since when did the FBI and the DEA start working together?" I couldn't help but cuss. Something wasn't right here.

"We're part of a covert operation authorized by the government. You're obstructing our operative. Don't get smart or we'll arrest you right here on the spot."

I looked around at all the Hollywood glitz and glamour and decided I didn't want to make a scene. That surely wouldn't be good for future business. "But what did I do?"

"We need you for questioning."

"Do you have probable cause?" I asked belligerently. "Do you have a warrant?"

"You either come with us or we'll make it hard for that brother of yours."

That's when I complied. What did they mean by that? "Hey, where are we going? Hey, what's going on?"

I climbed into an unmarked car. When they didn't jump on the Hollywood Freeway, and headed south on the Harbor Freeway, I knew we weren't headed to Parker Center, the central police station in the heart of downtown. We passed the Hollywood sign and it never seemed more ominous. The sky was clear of clouds, yet I felt a sharp pain in my old bullet wound. I touched the spot over my heart. Good indication there would be rain later that night.

Stumped, I rode in silence. My mind was spinning with questions. Was I being kidnapped? Who were these people? Were they legit? If not, what did they want with me? Then I had an even worse thought. Were they going to kill me? My hands suddenly turned clammy and adrenalin was coursing through my veins. Because Glass Eye was driving so fast, and changing lanes so often, the ride through the city felt like we were hammer sawing through traffic. We were driving at breakneck speed and the streetlights passed us in a blur.

A cyanide night sky covered L.A. and the ordinarily beautiful streetlights resembled dangerous satellites. L.A. is seductively beautiful like that. It's a pretty poison. Treacherous. For all its beautiful palm trees and exotic flowers, L.A. could be hell. While people were at the Academy Awards, someone on the other side of town was probably getting killed at this very moment. I cringed at the thought. I sure hoped that someone wasn't my brother. I shivered and held my arms at the elbows. Suddenly my dress felt too sheer to be out in the night air. Now I wished I'd never come to this awards ceremony.

Finally the car exited the Harbor Freeway, and I recognized that we were in the San Pedro industrial area. After a few quick turns on hilly streets, we pulled up into this small warehouse down near the docks, and I became afraid. I could smell the ocean nearby.

Who were these men? Were they really Feds? Were they going to kill me? My senses became super hyper-vigilant. I could already see myself sleeping with the fishes. Would I wind up a memory in the ocean?

Suddenly, the car screeched to a halt. We were in a darkened parking lot. The two men jumped out of the front seats, pulled me out of the car, and roughed me up; then they pushed me into an unmarked door of this warehouse. The smell of fish let me know I was at some type of fishing loading dock.

"What do you want with me?" I asked, feeling I had nothing to lose.

They didn't answer. The first thing they did was frisk me for a wire. Next, Glass Eye grabbed my purse. He opened it, snatched out the camera, and put it in his pocket. Obviously, he didn't recognize my phone because I had it in a case. Then they pushed me into a chair in an empty store room. I felt like I was a suspect, but what crime was I guilty of?

"I'll get straight to the point. We know you know where your brother is . . ."

"What are you talking about?"

"We know you know something. You're not a dummy."

"Did he get in touch with you?" Glass Eye interjected.

I crossed my eyes, looking crazy. "Do you have a chemical imbalance?"

"Don't get smart. We know all about you and what happened with those two officers. Just because you got off killing two officers before, you won't get away with it now. We got our eye on you."

"What are you talking about?" I pretended to be surprised.

They both hit me with a barrage of questions. "We know you know something."

"Did he get in touch with you?"

"Did who get in touch with me?" I kept my game face on. I didn't flinch a muscle. I'd learned over the years to never volunteer information. "I said I don't know what you're talking about."

"Don't get smart," Glass Eye snapped. "We know all about you and what happened with those two narcs you knocked off."

Agent Stamper jumped in. "Yeah, we know how you got fired. That you were a drunk. If we find out you had anything to do with Okamoto's murder, your ass is grass. He was a good man."

"Look. Okamoto was my friend. I've been cleared by IA, so you can stop talking all that yayo." Although I was afraid, they made me mad accusing me of killing my late partner, my friend.

"Well, time will tell. Anyhow, we know you know where the money is."

I paused. It was the money again. First Venita asked me about money and now two strange white men wanted to know about some money. "What money?"

"We gave your brother big money to go to Brazil."

"That doesn't even sound right."

"We were after the big fish. Diablo. Escobar, as he's calling himself these days. We have the Olympics coming to Rio de Janeiro in 2016 and we want to have things cleaned up by then. We wanted him to go and do the trade. We were going to catch Diablo this time with the money trail. Now the money has disappeared, and we don't know where your brother is."

"Why would you give him money like that?"

"You know your brother was a snitch. Rat, whatever you want to call it."

"I don't believe it."

"That's how he got out so early."

"Don't believe it." Everything in my spirit knew that didn't sound right.

"Well, you better believe it. Your brother is something else."

I couldn't say anything. I didn't have any idea who the man was Mayhem had become. We hadn't lived together since we were nine and ten, before we went into foster care.

"We know all about you too. If we find out you had anything to do with Okamoto's murder, we'll make sure you'll pay." This time it was Agent Braggs making the accusation, again, and I remained calm.

"Look, like I said, I've been checked out and I'm clean."

"Well, we know you know where the money is."

"What money are you talking about?"

"We had been following your brother. We don't want him. We want the big fish—Diablo."

"But why do you want me?"

"We understand your brother has been kidnapped."

"And?"

"He was working with us."

"What do you mean?"

"He turned state's evidence."

"You're lying. He'd never snitch."

"Whole bunch of people are snitches now if they don't want to spend time behind bars. He was working with us. Don't you think it was strange how he got out of prison on a ten-year bid?"

I didn't say anything. I remembered hearing that Mayhem's judge had overturned his sentence on a technicality. I heard all his last set of charges had been dropped so I decided to suspend disbelief on that one.

"Besides we got a lot of new charges on your brother. He's gone white collar crime."

"What?"

"He's involved in all types of money laundering schemes. Are you familiar with your brother's strip club and 'massage'"— he stopped and curled his fingers like quotation marks— "parlor in Hollywood? He even got the nerve to have pornography Web sites. He has a lot of money off shore in the Cayman Islands in some bogus account name that he's hidden away. He's also running an illegal cell phone business throughout the prison system. Even was trying to produce a rap group. So the IRS has a lot of charges waiting on him. Quite the entrepreneur."

I didn't say anything. This was all new to me.

"Hell, your brother is like the Steve Jobs of the streets now. This fool even has investments on Wall Street."

He's not too big of a fool, I thought. I was surprised myself. "And what does that have to do with me?"

"We know you're active on Twitter. We know you know the gangs on Twitter. And we know you're on Facebook. We know you keep your ear to the street."

"Look, I run a legitimate business."

"No, a lot of people know you're just like undercover and they work on your team and are willing informants."

"Not true." I shook my head.

Agent Stamper turned to Glass Eye and kind of snickered.

"Man, did you hear about how the gangs are doing drive-bys using Twitter to help them?"

"Yeah, yeah. You nig—I mean, you brothers make me sick. Just a bunch of savages. Animals, all of you. You all fuck up everything."

Boy, I wished I had a tape since white officers know they have to be politically correct now since Mark Fuhrman and the O.J. trial. My phone was in my purse so I couldn't get to it to push record.

In my heart, though, I didn't believe my brother was a snitch. Something was not adding up. But what I did know was someone ratted him out for him to get kidnapped.

My gut started thundering. It didn't take a rocket scientist to know that they were setting me up. But what did they want with me? Moreover, what was in it for them?

"So once again, where is the money?"

"What money?"

"We understand you will know how to get that. They say you can track anything."

"Who are 'they'?" I wasn't flattered at all.

"Look. We're going to keep busting your balls until you give up what you know."

"No, you're going to tell me something first. Do you know where my brother is?"

"Look, we can get that little license of yours pulled. I suggest you get busy and try to help us."

"Why should I?"

"We're part of a covert operation!"

"What do you mean?"

"We gave your brother five million to do a deal in Brazil. Now the money has come up missing and he's supposedly kidnapped. Do you have any idea where he is?"

"No. I don't keep up with my brother like that."

"He's going to pay unto Caesar what is due to Caesar. We're going to take you back now, but you better get busy. If you want to see your brother alive again, that is."

With that, they grabbed me from the chair, each taking an arm on one side, then deposited me in a rough toss like so much garbage into the back seat of the car. They both tossed me their cards, which I tucked in my purse.

"Give me back my camera."

"You'll get it back when we get that money."

"Hey, I paid a lot for that camera." It was the latest Canon and could even capture people in movement.

Neither man responded.

Thank goodness, I'd taken all my cases off the camera yesterday and only had shots of the Academy Awards.

They drove off, burning rubber. I guess I was safe for now . . . that was, if their wild driving didn't kill me first. I sat in the back seat, alone with my thoughts. I didn't know what my next move would be. What should I do?

Sometimes cases stick with you, take you dark places you don't want to go. Who was the bad guy in this case? I wondered. Was my brother such a bad person because he refused to not be able to take care of himself and his family? I didn't know what was right or wrong sometimes.

I'd made my share of mistakes in this life and I didn't want to judge my brother. I'd been fired from the LAPD due to my drinking problem, which I developed while on the job. I know I have to take full responsibility for my choice to drink, but what if I hadn't been able to use my skills to become a private investigator? What if I'd had to do something illegal to make a living? Then, how could I judge Mayhem?

Whenever I thought of my alcoholism, I saw my life in two acts. My life as an alcoholic was Act One and it was behind me. That was then. Act Two was now. I was sober now, one day at a time. I refused to let my past define me. Would I have done anything different if I could? I didn't know. My sponsor, Joyce, said our alcoholism can be a blessing if we turn our lives around and use it to help others. I didn't know about all that.

Now, fortunately, I was clean again, making a living. Wasn't I a free agent? The LAPD didn't sign my paycheck anymore. Internal Affairs didn't own me. A quiet voice spoke to me. *You are your own woman. You're self-employed. You can help your brother.*

Suddenly I recognized an emotion I was feeling. I was POed: pissed off. Red-hot rage pissed. I was furious that I couldn't go to the police for help. I was furious that these two jackasses didn't care what happened to my brother. I was furious that my brother was only considered a convict and not a human being. Maybe he didn't mean anything to them—to the world he was just another black man, dispensable. But, to me, he was my brother. They broke the mold when they made Mayhem.

He was the first male I'd followed around when I learned to walk. He was the one who taught me how to shoot a gun, and how to be as tough as a man. I remembered when we were kids, he'd said, "I'm going to teach you to shoot so you can take care of yourself so that no man can fuck over you like they do Mama." The truth of the matter was that there was only one man, Strange, our younger two siblings' father, who ever walked over my mother without her going to royal battle with him.

A couple of years ago, Venita had been released from prison after serving a twenty-year bid, so we were definitely not the Huxtables from *The Cosby Show*. My three siblings and I were raised in four different foster homes, except for Mayhem, who ran away and was on his own from the age of ten. I guessed that's why he was in the trouble he was in today.

I thought about my mother and how upset she was over the possible pending murder of her oldest son, her first born. She'd already lost her youngest two children. Up until this day, we didn't even know where my younger brother, Diggity, and my baby sister, Righteousness, were living, or if they were alive at all. We'd all spread to the four winds, it seemed. The younger two sibs seemed to have vanished into thin air. I was just trying to get my life together, and had two years of sobriety under my belt. I'd just started a search for my younger two sibs on the national registry, but no luck so far.

Something hit me. I realized I was alone in this world. Mayhem was all I had of my siblings and I didn't want to lose him. I didn't have to answer to a job, so I was free. I decided then and there I would return the money on the missing starlet to the family and handle my own family's business. But how?

Chapter Four

I didn't breathe easily until the two alleged federal officers dropped me back in front of the Kodak Theater near Hollywood Boulevard, hours later. I could see the crowds had cleared. Only a few stragglers remained in the area. The after parties were probably already in full swing. For some reason, it didn't bother me though. My mood was ruined after this night I'd had. Anyhow, I didn't feel like being around all the beautiful people right now. I didn't feel like watching Haviland act like a flibbertigibbet the way she did whenever she was in her element surrounded by other actors.

No, I just wanted to be alone. I had to process what had just happened. Who were these men? What did they want with my brother? What was this dad-blain money they were talking about? Was that the motive for kidnapping Mayhem?

A light mist began to fall softly, although it wasn't exactly raining. L.A. was funny like that. My old bullet hole, where either one of the two undercover cops—Flag, my ex, or Anderson, his partner-in-crime—had shot me always told the truth. Or, maybe I should say, my old wound never lied. It was going to rain sometime soon. That I knew for sure. If not tonight, by tomorrow for sure. My old wound was like an internal weather barometer.

At a loss as to what to do, I tottered over to Melrose Boulevard, ignoring how my feet hurt in the Prada heels I was wearing. I stopped before I reached Melrose, and slipped off my heels. I could feel the runs beginning up my light pantyhose as the sidewalk grated against my feet.

I started to call Romero but changed my mind. He probably was caught up on his own case. He'd been tagging a methamphetamine lab for some time now and he must have gotten a break in the case.

Finally I flagged down a cab. I decided I would go home to my garage apartment at my foster mother Shirley's and try to get some sleep. As I climbed into the cab, I turned on my phone and I saw I'd missed a lot of calls. I listened to my voice mail. The first call was from Venita. "We need you, Z. Please help us."

Several hysterical calls were from both Chica and Haviland. "Where are you?" they both screamed frantically into my message center. I decided not to return their calls at this moment. I didn't feel like being interrogated by them right now. Anyway, who did they think they were? My mama or something? Even my foster mother, Shirley, or my biological mother, Venita, didn't try to keep tabs on me.

I could only conjecture that things were crazy when Chica and Haviland realized I was missing from the Academy Awards ceremony. Absently, I told the cabbie where to transport me, which was home.

Before I could return my friends' calls, my phone rang, its Beyoncé song "Run the World (Girls)" ringtone startling me. I pushed answer and instantly a Skype picture of Mayhem appeared on my screen. I looked down and saw that this was Skype and was not a video. I gasped. I didn't know what to say. His eyes were swollen shut and blackened, but he was holding his head high.

"Hey, sis."

"Mayhem?" I didn't know what to say. "Are you okay?"

"For now. I need your help, sis."

"I—"

"I got caught slippin'. Go see Tank."

"Who's Tank?"

"My lieutenant. You've met him before. The big dude. He'll know what to do."

"Where is he?"

"Call Venita and get the number for him and set up a meeting."

"Why me, Mayhem?"

"You are trained. I'm counting on you, Z. You can do this."

"What do you want me to do?"

"Get the boys outta here."

My ears shot up.

"What boys?"

I thought he was talking about his muscle or his henchmen.

"My sons. They just kids," Mayhem said. "You've got to help me save my boys." He paused before continuing. "If they don't get this money they'll kill them too."

"Where is their mother?"

"They have their mama, my wifey, in Rio as a hostage."

"So what are you saying?"

"Sis, I'm going to need you to go to Brazil."

"What?" I almost screamed in the phone. He might as well have said he needed me to go to the moon. I swallowed a lump in my throat. "What's going on?

"I need you to go to get my wifey, Appolonia. Then the money can be released."

"What money? You're the third person who's mentioned this money."

"Just do it, bitch, if you want to see your brother alive again," an electronic squawk box voice interrupted, and Mayhem was cut off. The voice had sounded like a robot.

I didn't see the person on the screen but another threatening voice with the same electronic sound bellowed in the background, "The next time you see your brother it's going to be real bad. Tell your mother to get out her black dress if you don't get that money."

The line went dead. I tried to push redial but the number was unreachable.

For a moment I was too numb to move. Once I gathered my wits about me, again, I made sure my phone line was on, if the kidnappers decided to call back. I was so upset I needed to get my bearings.

Now Mayhem had said to call Venita, but I didn't want to call her. I was still mad at her for spending half my childhood in prison for a crime she didn't commit. I was not on exactly the best speaking terms with her, but then something occurred to me. Who else could I call? Mayhem asked that I call Venita. Our mother. She's the only person who would have Tank's contact information.

"Venita, it's Z."

My mother's voice sounded sleep filled, but I heard the alertness when she realized it was me. "Z?"

"I need Tank's phone number. Mayhem told me you would have it."

My mother was happy to hear from me, since I'd shut down my phone on her during our last contact via text. We didn't exactly have a close mother-daughter relationship, you might say. "I have his address too. He's in Imperial Courts."

I wrote down the phone number and address, then hung up. I could tell Venita was happy that I was on board. She didn't seem to realize something. Not only was he her first born, he was also my big brother. I wasn't doing this for her. I was doing this for Mayhem. Because when everything was all said and done, I remembered one thing: Mayhem killed for me when I was a child. The sad thing was, at the time, he was a child too. I was only nine and he was ten when the thing that destroyed our family happened. But I often wondered, what would have happened to me had he not pulled that trigger and killed Strange? I now wonder, where would I have wound up? Would my mother's then boyfriend, Strange, had molested me, the same way Chica's mother's boyfriend molested her throughout her early years before she was placed in foster care?

I thought about calling Romero, but changed my mind. After all, he was the law. Plus, he probably was out on his own surveillance case. We had an agreement never to interrupt each other when we were working.

Instead, I called my foster mother, Shirley, who had been the linchpin to love in my childhood and my adult life. The way safety pins used to hold old-fashioned cloth diapers together on babies, she'd held my life together when I was a nine-year-old child, traumatized from witnessing my father's murder, my mother's imprisonment, and the subsequent breakdown of our family system.

Two years ago, once again, Shirley had pulled my life together when I was a disgraced fired police officer, adult alcoholic, drowning in my own stew of demons. When I hit rock bottom, it was Shirley who climbed down in the cesspool of alcohol I was literally drowning in. She'd helped cleaned me up from my own vomit, sat through my detox, and got me into rehab until I could stand on my own two feet again. Up until then, I'd always thought I was so strong, but I found out I wasn't.

Sometimes when we can't pull things together or handle things, someone else has to hold our hand until we can handle them.

As soon as Shirley answered the phone, I felt a sense of comfort just hearing the sound of her voice. Unfortunately, just as I started my spiel, I realized I was talking to her voice mail. Daggonitt.

Anyhow what can she do? I asked myself inwardly. I didn't know, but I knew one thing for sure. Shirley was always the one to dust me off, and make me think I could make it.

That's why I needed to see her now. If anyone could make sense of this craziness, it would be Shirley.

I left a short, cryptic message. "Moochie, I can't talk on the phone about this. When I get home, can I come to talk to you? I know it's late, but I need to talk to you. It's urgent."

I always called Shirley by her nickname, Moochie, when I needed something.

Chapter Five

Just as I pulled up in front of Shirley's house, the rain had already stopped. It was just one of those capricious early spring showers that can hit L.A. one minute and disappear the next. The first thing I noticed was a black-and-white LAPD patrol car parked in the driveway, and, perhaps because I was already tense, I panicked. My antenna of "something bad is going on" rose up too high on my stress barometer and I could feel my hair standing at attention on my neck. My stomach knotted up. Was someone sick? Were Chica's girls okay? Lord, we couldn't take another hit emotionally since we'd lost Trayvon. I hated how I never relaxed anymore. I never took it for granted anymore that harm would never come to my loved ones anymore since Trayvon's death.

So why were the police at Shirley's at one in the morning? Something wasn't right. Baldwin Hills, one of the best-kept neighborhoods in L.A., was generally a quiet neighborhood, but this morning something was awry. The overhung streetlight was the only light on the street. From on top of the hill, I could still see the lights from the hill all over the L.A. Basin, but I felt like I was entering the Twilight Zone. Nothing seemed normal anymore.

"What's going on?" I asked, rushing up on Shirley, my heart galloping.

"He ran away."

"Who?"

"Daddy Chill. He's a wanderer risk now."

"I thought you said he'd plateaued," I said, uselessly, almost like an accusation. Just last week, on the phone, Shirley was bragging on how well Daddy Chill was doing.

"It's one step forward, two back. I found him missing from his room this afternoon. I just turned my back and he was gone."

"What?"

Shirley absently shook her head. She looked beyond disgusted. "They just found him about an hour ago. I don't know how much longer I can take this."

The two officers, one white and one black, were escorting my foster father, Daddy Chill, into the house. He had a "little boy lost" look on his face, one that was a bit befuddled, as he shambled his way into the front door. A sense of sadness swept over me, thinking of what a big, strapping man he used to be when he worked for the Post Office. Now he'd lost so much weight, he was so gaunt, so haggard, he was only a shell of the man he used to be. He was the one who had taught me to listen to my guts, which have really served me well as a private investigator.

"Hey, Z," Daddy Chill said sheepishly. He had a look on his face like a little boy who got caught stealing cookies out of the cookie jar.

"Hey, Daddy Chill." I reached over and hugged him. I could almost feel his bones through his shirt and it nearly broke my heart. He used to be a buff, muscular man. Now, combined with his gauntness, he felt like he was freezing cold. That's when I realized he didn't have on a jacket, and the night air in L.A., and the recent rain, could get deadly. A chill ran through me. He could've have frozen to death, out there, lost, and not knowing where he was.

"What happened?" I directed my question to Shirley.

Shirley's face was lined with worry and fatigue in a way I had never noticed before. With the melanin in her skin, she'd seemed ageless in the twenty-six years I'd known her. Now she looked even older than her sixty-one years.

"He got lost this afternoon. I've been driving around all over looking for him. I was supposed to wait for twenty-four hours to put in a missing person's report, so I wasn't able to get it in."

"Where was he?" I asked, following her into the house

"They just found him wandering in Culver City. He was wearing his I.D. bracelet, and that's the only way they knew how to get him back to me."

Oh, my God. So he'd been missing over half a day. His dementia had definitely gotten worse.

Shirley looked so distraught as she was pacing the floor. I could tell she was fit to be tied. "Oh, this man is giving me the blues." She wrung her hands as she led him into his bedroom.

After the two officers took the report and left,
I waited in the living room until Shirley medi-
cated Daddy Chill, so we could talk.

"Hi, Auntie Z."

I glanced up and saw Chica's oldest daughter,
Malibu, wander into the room. She reached up
and hugged me. She was rubbing her eyes.

"Did Papa Chill get back yet?" she asked
groggily, her pimpled face wrinkled from a
blanket of sleep and from an ongoing anxiety,
which made her seem far older than her years.
I hadn't seen her in a couple of weeks, since
I'd been crashing at Romero's lately, and she'd
blossomed over night. At thirteen, she could
pass for twenty. She had at least blossomed
from a B cup to a C cup in the past month, and
it was scary—what with all these sexual preda-
tors out there. I was glad she was with Shirley,
who really kept tight reins on Chica and me
when we were teens, but I didn't know about
now. Shirley seemed so drained from taking
care of Daddy Chill, I wondered how she could
take care of four budding girls, one of whom
was already a hottie.

"Yes, he's back. The police found him."

"What's wrong with him? He doesn't act like
himself."

"He has dementia, baby," Shirley said, re-
turning to the room.

"We hope he gets better." Nine-year-old
Soledad had joined her big sister. Her eyes
were alert, as if she'd never gone to sleep.

Shirley shook her head. She was generally
the optimist, but I guessed she was being the
realist. "His disease is progressive."

"What does that mean?"

"It's not going to get better." Her voice sounded flat and blunt.

Both girls opened their mouths into round Os and started crying in big gulps. Shirley reached out and hugged them. "Oh, calm down, girls. I'm sorry I said it like that. Everything is going to be all right."

"Is Papa Chill going to die like Trayvon did?" Soledad asked between sniffing and huffing.

"No, I'm just tired, girls. He can live a long time with the disease. Don't worry. He will be all right."

"Shirley, where are Charisma and Brooklyn?" Those were Chica's younger two daughters who were respectively eight and six.

"They went to spend the night with Chica while I looked for Chill." Chica kept the girls every other weekend now that she'd been clean and sober.

Shirley went to comfort the girls and put them back to bed. I sat in the living room, alone with my doubts and my fears. *What should I do?* Why did I have to get involved? And, if I did, would I be able to help my brother? Wouldn't this be dangerous? This case was too big for me.

I leaned my head back against the wing-back chair and absently looked around the room. I was comforted by the same antique Victorian sofa sitting in the same corner. The familiar fragrance of potpourri sitting in a vase filled my nostrils. I felt comforted when I gazed at my high school cap and gown graduation picture, which was placed next to Chica's high school graduation picture on the fireplace mantel.

This made me feel like I had a point of reference. Some shared history. Home. This was home for me—the former foster kid. People didn't understand how much that meant to me. There were no pictures of my childhood before I stayed with Shirley. I only had one picture of me as a baby with my father that my mother had salvaged while she was on lockdown. To this day, I still often perused Shirley's many photo albums, which captured pictures of our childhood vacations, the teenaged guerilla theater, or beauty contests Chica and I had participated in, and both junior high and high school graduation.

Finally Shirley came out of the bedroom. "How are the girls doing?" I asked.

"They're in counseling. They still haven't gotten over Trayvon. I don't think I'll ever get over him either." Shirley shook her head, her face growing drawn and pinched. Her eyes still carried a wounded look, over a year after Trayvon's murder. He'd been her pet of all the foster grandchildren.

"Yes, we all miss him." Chica's son had really been a good kid. Being the only boy, his four surviving sisters still missed him.

"How was the Academy Awards? That dress is beautiful. You look stunning!" Shirley said, as if she was just noticing for the first time that I was wearing after-five apparel.

"It was different. But two Feds pulled me out and I didn't get to stay for the awards ceremony or the after parties."

A look of alarm crossed Shirley's face and her tone changed. "You left a message that you needed to talk. What's the matter?"

I told her my dilemma. I finished spilling out my story, filled with doubts and recriminations that I hadn't reacted sooner. I waited for her to say something. "Shirley, what should I do?"

Shirley reached out and took my hand. She held it to my chest. She was silent for what seemed like the longest time, but was probably only seconds. "Do you hear your heartbeat?"

I nodded.

"There's no one else's in the world like yours. Just listen to it . . . In your silent moments you'll know what to do. Follow your heart, baby."

"I want to, but . . ." I faltered.

"But what?"

"I'm scared."

"Scared of what?"

"I guess I might as well tell you. I'm scared if I stick my neck out, I might get hurt. These people don't play."

"We all have to help people. What kind of world would this be if no one ever helped one another?"

I thought of all the children Shirley had helped, including me. Where would I be if she hadn't taken me in as a foster child when I was young? "I'm afraid, though. I don't know what I might find."

"Okay, what would you feel if you don't at least try to help?"

I thought about it for a minute. I reluctantly had to admit something. "I guess I'd feel awful. My brother said his sons are not even safe and he wants me to help get them somewhere safe."

"Just remain true to yourself. I can't promise you that it will work out, but it will work better for you if you do what is in you to do."

"I wish it were that simple. This thing could be dangerous. We're talking Crips, cartels, Feds. I don't know what's going on."

Shirley closed her eyes and prayed out loud a prayer she knew word-for-word by heart.

> *In the Lord, put I my trust. How say ye to my soul. Flee as a bird to your mountain? For, lo, the wicked bend their bow, they make ready their arrow upon the string, that they may privily shoot at the upright in heart. If the foundations be destroyed, what can the righteous do? The Lord is in his temple, the Lord's throne is in heaven; his eyes behold, his eyelids try, the children of men. The Lord trieth the righteous: but the wicked and him that loveth violence his soul hateth.*
>
> *Upon the wicked he shall rain snares, fire and brimstone, and a horrible tempest; this shall be the portion of their cup. For the righteous Lord loveth righteousness; his countenance doth behold the upright.*

"That's beautiful! What prayer is that, Moochie?"

"Psalm 11. This will help you triumph over adversity."

"I don't know," I said, still not certain prayer could help in this case.

Shirley stood up. "Think of David and Goliath. Go with God." Shirley hugged me. "I love you, Z."

"Love you too, Moochie."

I hugged her back and got up to leave. I barreled inside my garage apartment and threw on a pair of black jeans, a black T-shirt, and jacket. I packed my piece on my shoulder strap. I always felt safer on the streets with my pearl-handled Glock. I fed my ferret, Ben, and let him out his cage so he could be free to roam my studio apartment. I didn't know how long this day was going to be. After our postprandial lovemaking session, I'd taken a long nap the afternoon before at Romero's so that helped. I called Romero to tell him I wasn't coming to spend the night at his place after all, and it went to his voice mail. I left a brief message.

My thoughts turned back to my brother. I didn't even have any childhood pictures of us together. Now I only had the image of Mayhem on my phone screen, eyes blackened and swollen. My eyes watered, but I bit my lip to keep from crying. Was I my brother's keeper? I guessed I was.

I tried to call the number Venita had given me for Tank, but I didn't get an answer. There was no voice mail system set up, and I wouldn't have left a message anyhow. I hung up, clearly

shaken, but an invisible hand pushed me forward. It was four in the morning when I headed
to Imperial Courts. It looked like it was going to
be a long night.

Chapter Six

Crossing the bridge into Imperial Courts in Watts, my hands felt clammy as I gripped the steering wheel and a dull thud stabbed me in my stomach. My intestines growled and felt all twisted up. My gut was saying that this was going to be dangerous. That wasn't a good sign. My gut never lied.

At first I felt this dropping sensation from my chest to my stomach, and then my heart went into a full throttle of arrhythmia. I did a series of deep breathing just to slow my heart rate down. My tae kwon do instructor, Mr. Wong, always said to breathe deeply before going into battle. I guessed I was going to have to go to war. Unfortunately, I didn't know who the enemy was.

I wanted to back out, but something compelled me forward. I knew my life would change if I even talked to Tank. Then I'd be committed, and once I was in, I'd be all the way in, even if it meant my death. Oh, no! My feelings flip-flopped. Hell naw. I was back to cussing again. *I should turn this car around and go back home.* I had too much to lose. I was just beginning to get a toehold on life again since I'd lost my police job. The PI jobs were coming in steadily where the good months carried me over the slow months.

My mind stayed in a battle with the pros and cons of getting involved. Here I was even thinking about the new American Dream of becoming a reality show star. I didn't need this drama in my life. But then, Mayhem's blackened eyes would come back and haunt me all over again. No, I had to do whatever I could do within my power to help my brother. He was all I had of my siblings.

I called Tank several times more to no avail. I started to turn back around, but my mind wouldn't let me. Now I was curious and I was compelled to go forward. Where was Tank? Did he set my brother up? Wasn't he supposed to be his lieutenant?

What was going on? Why did Mayhem want me to go to Brazil? What could Tank tell me? I needed more information and the only way I could get it was to go see Tank.

As I drove through the outhouse dark streets, I saw the differences from Baldwin Hills, less than twenty miles away. Graffiti marking different gang territories let me know on whose turf I was treading. Bullet holes left their marks on different walls, houses, and cars too.

I realized that I was entering what was an entire subculture—the other America. I was born into it, but through a twist of fate, somewhat escaped it. After being raised in foster care from age nine, somewhere along the way, I decided I couldn't live like this. Petty, low-level crime. Gangbanging. The world of get-money chicks. Sheesh.

My mother was a Crip—a gangbanger—until she went to prison. Now she was still a respected OG. No, I had to break the cycle.

For years I carried survivor's guilt, but now I felt like an ambassador. I was like a spy who could slip in and out of corporate America, then go back to the underworld. Although we had a black president, for too many of my people things had not changed. The recession, unemployment, things for many had not gotten better; they'd just had gotten worse. The Black middle class's grip on its lifestyle was tenuous, to say the least. People seemed to be slipping into darkness.

I couldn't even say if it was a good thing or bad, but some men refused to be out of work. Men like my brother. They created work for themselves and others—even if it was on the wrong side of the law.

Thinking of it, I noticed something. Now that I was in South L.A., a sense of danger quivered in the air. I smelled it and I could taste it. I could feel the tension between the gangs and the police cars, which prowled the streets all night. Yet, at the same time, I personally felt an alliance to my people. I felt like I was entering a colonized state. A police state. With the fading middle class, some of the denizen had slipped into a permanent underclass status, but these are my people and I have to help and defend them where I can. Besides, I could get into cracks the police couldn't get in.

Why? Because I spoke the language of the hood. I knew it because I grew up the first nine

years of my life in nearby Jordan Downs Projects.

Ebonics was a language, and like any first
language, you had to grow up hearing it to understand all its subtleties and nuances. There
was a rhythm and a poetry to the language of
the street. It changed and grew every day in
an ongoing effort to continue to dupe the law.
And it always amazed me how the language
lost its punch when I hear it bastardized by
mainstream America. Even newscasters tried
to speak in hip hop these days.

My car was old and I didn't have a naviga-
tion system, so I relied on my memory of the
Watts streets' layout. I felt a sense of unease
in the people who were out this time of night
as I drove up the street. Unless you were in
the 5 percent oligarchy, you were like the rest
of us, who were living in a time of uncertainty.
People who once held six-figure salaries no
longer had them. Unemployment benefits had
been extended beyond twenty-four months—
a benefit that was previously unheard of—
and still there were not enough jobs. Middle-
class America had taken up in arms and was
Occupying Wall Street all over the country.
The whole world had changed overnight for
us Americans. In a crazy way I understood
how the man I'd read about in the paper felt,
who, after having been Harvard educated, and
a former Wall Street investor, was now rob-
bing banks. He probably felt like the bottom
had fallen out and he had nothing to lose. The
world, including mortgages, was upside down

and people were losing homes to foreclosures like houses under water during a tsunami.

Regardless of what was going on, everyone was in search of that elusive American Dream. People were desperate, and desperate men would do what they had to do to eat. I had to assume this had been Mayhem's stance all along—even before the economy crashed.

I guessed I'd already been through my own peripeteia—the point when everything the heroine thought she knew about life was wrong. The point when my American Dream and my ideal job were snatched out from under me like a double whammy rug, leaving me to fall on my big posterior. Yes, I'd lost my hard-won job as a police officer, and had gone through the shame and degradation of being a drunk who hit bottom. But with my loved ones' help, I'd worked hard to build my life back. And this time around, it was better than before. So I really had a lot to lose, even looking into this case.

As early as it was, the crackheads filled the gray streets. People who looked old beyond their years shuffled up and down the streets. Strawberries trying to hook up with tricks stalked the boulevards. Their hips swiveled dangerously as they teetered up and down the stroll in high stilettos. Most of the working girls wore almost nonexistent short skirts, which resembled tube tops and string-like halter tops, although it was forty degrees outside. Some gangbangers, pants hanging low and showing their boxer shorts, leaned on corners, waiting to sell their next bag. The sounds of sirens played in the backdrop like beats to a rap song.

I finally located the address, deep within the projects. It was a single-story stucco bungalow. I looked around and pulled my Glock out and put it to my side. I approached the door, paused, then knocked.

"Who is it?" a baritone male voice barked.

"Z. I met you before. Mayhem sent me. I tried to call you."

I saw his light brown iris squint as he looked directly into my eyes from out of the peephole.

"Ain't you One time?" One time was the street phrase for the police in L.A.

"Not anymore."

Slowly, the door cracked, sending out just a shard of light onto the porch.

"So you're boss man's baby sis." He said it more as a statement than a question.

Finally, he opened up what sounded like a dozen deadbolt locks. He was strapped, and pointed his gun from side to side on the door. He craned his neck, looked around the corner, and pulled me in.

I put my Glock back into my sling-shot, which hung under my arm. Once inside, I got my first good look at Tank. I was so afraid the first time I met him at one of Mayhem's spots, I didn't really get a good once-over of him. He wore a close fade haircut. He really didn't look like Michael Clarke Duncan. He was just big like him—like a Mandingo slave who was bred by the former slave owners to be strong enough to build this country on his back.

This early morning he wore a wife beater, which revealed an old bullet wound on his huge left bicep and what looked like a razor slice across his throat, which had miraculously healed in a large wormy keloid. Just seeing his battle wounds made me unconsciously touch my old bullet wound above my heart and I experienced a sharp stab of pain just from the memory. The irony was I was shot in the line of duty by so-called "friendly fire" from my two officer colleagues trying to cover up their corruption.

"Yes, I'm Mayhem's sister."

"What do you want?"

"Mayhem sent me to you. He said you would know what to do."

"Okay. C . . . cc . . . could you show me some I.D. or something?" This was the second time hearing him speak, and I'd never realized he was a stutterer. But maybe he was just nervous.

"Why? Don't you remember when I came back and saw Mayhem last year?"

"I can't exactly remember what you looked like. You've lost weight or something."

I pulled out my private eye badge. True; I had trimmed down since taking tae kwon do, and I was wearing my hair longer.

"Okay, now I remember you. You've fallen off some. I remember you being thick."

I flexed my muscles, which were still small, but more defined. "Working out. Okay? Am I straight with you?"

"Yeah, come on in. Things are getting hot around here. Got to get off the street. Are you strapped?" he asked me as one more precaution.

"Yes, but I'm not here to hurt you. I'm here to try to help my brother."

As soon as I stepped into the living room of a home, I inspected the room in a cursory glance. It looked like it was a typical project home: swamp-colored carpet, matching pleather loveseat and sofa, fake leopard-skin and giraffe-print throw pillows, fake wood table and étagère, cheap wall prints of Malcolm X and Martin Luther King, Jr. The only difference in this living room and the many living rooms I'd been in were the two computers on the table pushed over in the corner. A TV blared in the corner.

"Could you cut the TV off?" Okamato, who was also my trainer, had taught me to shut off all TVs to keep from being ambushed when you stepped into a home. You never knew what danger lurked under the noise of that TV. Urban legend had it that a police had been stabbed from an unknown party in the house while the TV was playing *The Price is Right*.

Tank sauntered across the floor and complied by pushing the remote. For a big man, he was light on his feet, like a linebacker. I kept my back to the door, another habit I learned as a policewoman. Meanwhile, I scoped all the corners. We appeared to be alone, except for a blue pit bull sitting in the doorway of what I assumed was a kitchen. He looked poised to attack.

"Sit, Killer," Tank ordered. The dog sat back on his haunches, and settled down.

"Anyone else in the house?"

"No."

My back was ramrod straight, and all my senses stood at attention as I did whenever I felt the need to be on point. I started to ask for Tank to lock up the dog, but changed my mind. The dog seemed docile around his owner.

I got straight to the point. "Who set my brother up?"

"I don't know exactly."

"Back to my question. Did you rat him out?"

I thought about how many times lieutenants betrayed their leader for the enemy's side.

"Hell naw. Me and Big Homie go way back. W. . . www . . . we got jumped into the Crips together when we was twelve. He like a brother to me. He my nigga. My dog."

Tears glistened in Tank's eyes, which was kind of touching in such a bear of a man, and I kind of felt like he was telling the truth. But something made me hold back my trust. I needed answers first. "What happened to my brother then?"

"I swear on everything I love, I didn't have anything to do with it. Like I said, I was doing a run that day. I believe Big Homie was set up by someone else."

"Who?"

"As I said, I was gone makin' a run for Big Homie. The person who was supposed to make the run called in sick."

"What is his name?"

"Playboy."

"What happened to him?"

Tank didn't answer.

I pressed the issue. "Where is he at now? I want to talk to him."

"We won't have to worry about him no more."

A chill raced through me when he said this, but I had to stay on point about my brother. Now I remembered I was in the jungle. This was one of the laws of the jungle. There were laws you abided by in that jungle. I thought of the word on my crossword puzzle I was working the day before. Quisle: to betray, especially by collaborating with an enemy.

"Did you find out who took my brother?"

"It was an ambush. One of our men who got away saw them. I didn't see who took him, but I think it's a Mexican cartel. They say they were wearing face masks, too."

"What makes you think they were Mexican if they were wearing masks?"

"They had a Mexican accent."

"How about the tattoo?"

"The Eses wear those. According to J-Rod, the one that got away, they come from a family. From what one of my boys who got away said, one wore this strange tattoo that had a cobra wrapped around a pole."

"About what time did this happen?"

"It happened about two in the morning last night."

I knew that was an unusual tattoo. I'd already learned on another case there was a special tattoo parlor in downtown L.A. that specialized in unusual tattoos.

"Do you think my brother's a snitch?"

He shook his head. "H . . . h . . . hell naw! Who told you that?"

"I'm trying to rule out something that was told to me."

"Look, he did several bids where he could have taken people down and he didn't."

"What did he want me to come to you for? He said you would know what to do."

Tank paused, before speaking. "Okay, Z, this is important. You've got to get Mayhem's kids. If you don't, they may get murked."

"Wait. Slow down. This is a lot of information for me to digest. First things first. Where are my nephews?"

"They're with my sss . . . sister. Them li'l niggas be wilding out, so please hurry and get 'em. Here's her address." He handed me a note. "Name's Rena Holt. She's in Bellflower. Here's a note to give 'er from me to let her know you are who you say you are. You've got to get them kids out of Cali, though."

"Okay." I felt numb.

"Something else, though. Mayhem told me to set this up for you. I talked to him last night. Here's a passport; you'll just have to put a recent picture in it. And here's a ticket to Rio de Janeiro. You're gonna need a tetanus shot, a ten-year vaccine for yellow fever, and a prescription. That's on that note too, with a doctor's name and address; he'll see you right away."

I looked down and saw the sister's address, a doctor's name and address in Hollywood, and the name of an antimalarial drug, Lariam.

"What? Slow your roll. Why Brazil?"

"This thing is big. Big Homie was going to do a deal in Brazil. But somehow Appolonia wound up goin', I guess 'cause she knew the language. Anyway, now, they holding her hostage. The money that was going to go on the deal can be used to release Big Homie.

"You've got to leave tomorrow afternoon. Make sure you get this prescription and the shots for yellow fever."

"Why?"

"You'll be near the Amazon. A woman named Esmeralda will meet you at the airport. She'll have a sign. Here's a picture of Appolonia."

I glanced down at the photo of an attractive Brazilian woman. She had thick auburn curly shoulder-length hair, a rich bronze complexion, and full lips, which seemed to sneer out at the world. She had a small beauty mole on her upper lip, and almond-shaped eyes, which gave her a sultry look. She had the sheer dazzle and glamour of the late Elizabeth Taylor—except with that South American beauty factor combined. Yes, she looked like the type of eye-candy woman Mayhem would want as a trophy wifey on his arm. "What's her last name?"

"Silva. I don't mean to rush you, but you really need to get your nephews somewhere safe."

"Has there been a direct threat against the kids?"

"They want all three of 'em. They got a hit out on 'em."

"What can I do with them?"

"Just get them somewhere safe before you leave the country. You'll find them with my sister. You've got to get them out of L.A."

By now my heart was beating a maniacal rhythm up against my rib cage, I was so upset.

"I want to show you something." He went over to the computer and flipped it on. "I think this where all the damn trouble began. Mayhem had a lot of Web sites that was doing good. He'd even started investing in stocks and bonds on Wall Street. That's when the Feds and everybody started coming down on him.

"Then these bloggers started talkin' shit 'bout him because he was tryin' to get a rap group out there. The bloggers the ones get beef going with people. Then they go sit on they ass behind their keyboards and laughin' at niggas. I . . . I told Big Homie this Internet ain't nothin' but the devil's playground, but, naw, he said this was the new way of doin' business."

I was surprised how quickly Tank's sausage fingers could type. I waited while he pulled up accounts, opened them, then closed them and saved the information to a flash drive.

"These are just some of Mayhem's accounts. This is the one you'll have to have the money transferred to. It's also the one you can draw money out of for your trip and your services. I'll call you if I find out anything else. I got your number in my cell."

"Thanks," I said.

"Hey, you're fam. Family take care of each other."

Chapter Seven

The purplish cast of a breaking aurora gave way to a mauve overcast morning as I drove to Bellflower. I tried to map out what I would do with the boys once I found them. My heart was pounding and I felt myself hyperventilating. The rivaling drug dealers would shoot babies, women, and children. Just as in war time, women and children were collateral damage. The cartels didn't believe in leaving any witnesses behind, either. In the case of male children, they didn't want the boys to grow up and seek revenge.

I picked up my speed and jumped on the 105 freeway. *Okay, calm down,* I assured myself. *The boys will be fine.* Then a strange thought hit me: if I got the boys, where would I take them? *Should I call Department of Children and Family Services? The Child Abuse hotline who can alert Child Protective Services?* If I couldn't find anyone to take them, what was I going to do with some kids? That's why I never had any in the first place. As much as I loved Romero, I didn't even try to do the stepmama thing with his six-year-old daughter, Bianca.

How old were my nephews anyhow? Were they in diapers? Toddling? Walking? But, no, they must be older if Mayhem had described them as "thuglets" last year. Tank even said they "be wilding out."

I put in my earplugs so I wouldn't get a ticket for driving while talking on a cell phone. I pushed my speed dial and called Shirley. "Oh, this man is running me crazy," was almost the first thing out of her mouth. No "Hello, Z"; no "Kiss my toe"; no "Kiss my foot." Just straight rambling. She *was* stressed out.

"Since he got back from running away, he's throwing fits. He wants to wander around the house all night. I had to stay up with him all night. I'm exhausted."

"Oh, Shirley. You poor thing. I feel bad I can't help you. I might have to go out of the country."

I could tell Shirley was so upset she didn't even really register what I'd said. I hung up, feeling defeated. I guessed I wouldn't be able to bring the children there for respite until she could get them somewhere. Shirley was in need of respite herself.

The sun was burning off some of the morning fog as soon as I arrived at the Cape Cod–style cottage belonging to Tank's sister, Rena. She was a thirty-something fair-skinned woman. She wore her hair in locks. She was small boned, quite a contrast to her brother. She looked both exhausted yet relieved to see me. From her uniform I assumed she was a nurse. "I'm glad to see you. I just got in from work. I'm a CNA. I work nights at a nursing home and this is already getting to be too much."

I guessed Tank had alerted her that I was on my way to pick up the boys.

As soon as I set eyes on the three boys, my long-lost nephews, I knew they were my brother's children. They each looked like various shades of what I remembered of Mayhem when we were children. One had his long slope head, another one had his full lips, and the youngest one had his pudgy nose. They were well-built, muscular children. Although I remember Mayhem saying he had three different baby mamas, the boys all looked like him. The oldest wore his hair shoulder length, the middle one had a Mohawk, and the youngest son wore a shag haircut. They were all well dressed, wearing Sean John's outfits. They sported what looked like brand new Nikes, too. I didn't like the earring pierced in the oldest boy's ear. I couldn't tell how old they were because of the hardened looks in their eyes. I felt a sense of kinship akin to how slaves had to feel after Emancipation when they reconnected with long-lost relatives. Inside I was elated, but that sense of elation was soured quickly.

"Who are you?" The oldest demanded with the same brash confidence that Mayhem possessed when he was a child. He was bowlegged and stood with his legs arched back the same way Mayhem used to do.

"I'm your Auntie Z."

"My daddy ain't never tell us nothin' about-'chu." This little defiant man-child even had his mouth twisted up the way my brother used to do, too.

I suppressed a grin. "Well, he told me about y'all."

I recalled my first meeting with Mayhem after fifteen years. He'd referred to his sons as his "little thuglets" and I could see why. The oldest one already had what I presumed was a battle scar on the right side of his face. An inch higher and it would have put out his eye. The two-inch keloid glared against his fair complexion. The way he acted though, this little man wore this scar as a badge of honor.

That's when I realized I didn't know any of their names. "What are your names?"

"How you s'posed to be somebody auntie and you don't even know our name," the oldest bleated in my face.

"Well, I am your auntie," I said firmly. "That's a good question." I showed Tank's note to Rena.

Rena, who had receded into the background after she let me in, spoke up. "Their names are Milan, Koran, and Tehran. Milan is ten, Koran is nine, and Tehran is seven."

"Okay, Milan, Koran, and Tehran, I'm your Auntie Z. You're coming with me." To break the awkwardness, I gave them each a hurried hug, which none of them responded to, but what did I expect? I was a stranger to them. We were tied by blood, yet, at the same time, we were separated by years and distance.

A faint sadness swept over me. How many more families had been separated because of this madness—gangs, prison, drugs? As I huddled the still disgruntled boys into my car, with their backpacks, I wondered where I could take them. Then I had a thought: why not at least try Shirley, despite my earlier reservations?

But almost as soon as I thought it, I realized Shirley really was out of the question. Besides, she had protective custody of all four of Chica's girls, and having prepubescent, mannish boys in the same age group probably wouldn't be a good idea. Plus, she had restrictions with her foster care license. Girls and boys couldn't sleep in the same room and her rooms were all full.

That's when I thought of Venita. At first, I thought that was a crazy idea. How could I even consider my biological mother? Hey, she didn't even finish raising us. But then I thought about it. After all, she was their grandmother. This could be her redemption. Perhaps this would give her a second shot at being a mother. She sure messed up with us.

And, as much as I hated to admit it since I didn't want to forgive her yet, she was different now—in a good way. Maybe she could give her grandchildren what she wasn't able to give us: a suitable, stable home. She was now clean and sober. She had slowly rebuilt her life since her release a year ago. Against all odds of recidivism, prison had rehabilitated her, or so it would seem.

Why shouldn't she take her own grandchildren? But would she want to take them now that she was free and living her own life?

Chapter Eight

I pulled over to a curb, and stepped out the car so I could call Venita and talk in private. I didn't want to scare the boys, although they didn't look like you could frighten them easily. I wondered if they knew their lives were in danger.

My mother answered on the first ring, as if she was waiting by the phone, expecting a call from me. I could tell she was both happy and surprised to hear my voice. At the same time, I could hear the relief in her voice.

"Are you going to help?" she asked eagerly.

"Do I have a choice?" I knew it was a rhetorical question.

"What can I do to help?"

"Can you take Mayhem's kids?"

"Sure. Bring them babies to me." There was no hesitation in her voice and I felt a smidgen of jealousy.

"They're not babies and they are a handful. They're just like Mayhem."

Shirley chuckled. "I can handle them."

"Well, you're going to have to get them out of L.A. They're in danger. Whoever has Mayhem will kill them if they find them. Are you off parole yet?"

"Yes."

"Good. Do you have any money to get out of the state?"

"David set up an account for me about six months ago. I still have the money because of my job." She said the word "job" with pride. That's right, Venita worked at a floral shop. First time in her life my mother had held down a job, and from what I could see, she'd been a good employee over the past year. Before she went to prison, she'd always been a welfare queen and sugar daddy baby.

For a moment, I felt a stab of jealousy in my stomach, though, when she called Mayhem by his real name, but then I remembered Venita gave up twenty years of her life for my brother when she took the fall for the murder her ten-year-old child committed. I'd always known he was her favorite, even when we were little. All because he was a boy.

To mask my feelings of sibling rivalry, I became brusque. "Well, this is the time to use the money. You've got to get out of town today and take his boys with you. Can you do that?"

"I'll do whatever I have to do."

"Do you need a ride to the bus station or train station? Do you have someplace you can go?"

"I know where I can take them. No, I can catch a cab. You need to get moving to try to help David."

I felt a little envy again when I hung up. *Help David.* That was my birth mother's first concern. *Help her first born.*

In an ideal world, she would have said, "Thanks for sticking out your neck to help my criminal son and his underworld mess," but I guess that was in a dream world. This was the real world.

I climbed back into the car.

"Where we goin'?" Milan demanded.

"I've got a surprise for you," was all I said. The boys and I drove in silence to Venita's colonial in View Park. I hadn't been to her place before, but I knew her address. I was thinking about my mother. She'd come up in the world in a short time. A year ago she was living in a halfway house. Now she was living in what was an old, settled middle-class Black neighborhood in South Los Angeles. I guess the same way the NBA players looked out for their moms, Mayhem had looked out for Venita. But could he buy her back twenty years of her life? Did they ever discuss what went on between them? I wondered.

I hustled the boys out of the car, all the time looking over my shoulder. I rushed up the brick walkway and banged on her heavy mahogany door.

"Is that you, Z?" Venita called through the door. She peered through her peephole and snatched open the door.

As soon as Venita saw the boys, she broke into tears, grabbed all three boys at once, and began to kiss them all over their faces. She held all three of them in a headlock embrace. I was shaken. I'd never seen my OG Cripping mama cry before. I guess time brings about a change.

"Leave us alone with all that mush," Koran said, pushing Venita away.

"Who is you anyway?" Tehran demanded, lip curled in defiance.

"Yeah, we're not babies. We're soldiers." Milan stood with his shoulders back, bandy legs arched, like he was one of those Ugandan children soldiers.

"Now you see how bad this Crip thing is, Venita?" I shook my head in distaste.

Venita ignored me. "Boys, I'm your grandmother."

"No, you ain't. My grandmother in Brazil."

"My grandma live in Arleta."

"My grandma live in Southgate."

"Well, I'm all y'all daddy's mama. Y'all may have different mamas, but y'all all got the same daddy. He my son. Y'all all look just like that boy."

"I thought his old lady was in jail," Koran scoffed.

"I'm his old lady, and I'm here. Do I look that old to you?"

"Yeah," Tehran piped up. "You *real* old."

I cringed. I remembered how vain Venita used to be, and with her new Rihanna-red weave and super long fake acrylic nails, she still thought, at fifty-one, she was quite a diva, even if a ghettofabulous one. Venita's mouth crumpled and I could tell she was hurt.

"Hey, Tehran." I stepped in to soften his childish, outspoken blow. "You need to take charm lessons from your daddy. Now take Mayhem. He was a charmer, even when he was a little boy."

"You got that right. He sho was," Venita said, eyes glazing over with her happy memories of my brother's childhood before she went to prison.

We stepped inside the living room. The house boasted light rosewood floors. A new, expensive-looking French provincial sofa and loveseat sat in the corner. The boys sat down. For all their bravado, the boys seemed at ease with Venita. I guess game recognizes game.

"So you really *is* our daddy mama?" Milan asked, kind of with curiosity, kind of in awe. Apparently, Mayhem had told them about Venita and how her street reputation preceded her. If there was such a thing as being a ghetto celebrity, well, then Venita had been that back in the day. Whipping police's assess, shooting, riding on drive-bys with the men, the whole bit.

"Yeah. I sure am. What else you wanna know?"

"I wanna know was my daddy a Crip when he was my age?"

"Sure was."

"Well, why don't he want us to be one? Talkin' 'bout he wants us to go to college and work on Wall Street. Talkin' 'bout how that's really gangsta."

I was tickled myself at that. Mayhem may have been a criminal, but he was telling his boys the truth about that. More companies, countries, and Savings and Loans had been derailed by white collar crime than street crime could ever touch.

However, Venita ignored their questions. "Come on in and eat some grits and toast. Your daddy loved grits when he was a boy."

"Venita, you're gonna hafta get out of dodge—soon!" I urged. "Y'all can do the grandma-grandson thang once you get settled."

"Okay, okay, but they got to eat something. We'll be out of L.A. by two this afternoon. There's a Greyhound I can take."

"I don't care where you go but make sure it's not Atlanta or a big city where they can be traced. Change your phone number, and call me from a phone card when you get wherever you're going."

I said my good-byes and awkwardly hugged my nephews. As I turned to leave, Venita reached up and hugged me.

"Thanks, Z. I know this is a lot. . . ."

Reluctantly, I hugged her back. I guess we had a new bond. We were both getting ready to descend into hell together.

I didn't breathe easily until I left the boys in Venita's care. I felt like she was strong in a way that I'd never be strong. Like the fact she'd had babies and survived being separated from them, yet still could have hope at a second chance at life.

I still wouldn't feel right until I got word they were safe out of the state. Somewhere. Anywhere. I didn't even care. Anywhere but here.

Chapter Nine

After I left Venita's, I decided to go and sniff around before I went to the doctor in Westwood.

I called and scheduled the so-called quack doctor's appointment for later that afternoon, but I wanted to check out a few leads. First, I planned to go to the jungle. I decided to contact F-Loc since he was an OG who kept his ear to the pulse of the streets.

It was noon by the time I drove up Crenshaw Boulevard, heading for the jungle, which was off Martin Luther King Boulevard. Driving along, I took in the L.A. sights and sounds. The feel of an open African market was palpable. Black Muslim brothers from the Nation of Islam sold the *Final Call* magazine and the famous bean pies. Vendors had set up on street corners selling incense, cheap paintings, imitation Oriental rugs, and various goods. A few local authors were even selling their books from stands they set up on the corner. I couldn't knock an honest hustle though.

This was a neutral territory. First, you have to understand something. L.A. has an invisible grid covered with gangs. You have to know the streets, and the terrain, to know which terri-

tory you're in or you could wind up in a world
of trouble. Just one street in the wrong direction could mean your life. Thank goodness, I
knew Bloods' territory, Crips' territory, and
the different Mexican gang areas. You even
had Asian gangs to contend with in L.A. Many
of the foreign gangs started out as protection
groups because they were immigrants, but they
grew into gangs and cartels once the drug trade
became involved. Each gang had its own loyal-
ties, its own turfs to protect. Most of the turfs
were to be protected for money and for com-
merce.

Then you had the other 95 percent of working stiffs, people who, like me, lived out their
lives in relative peace until a member of their
family was killed or got on crack. This is how
I became a PI in the first place: when Trayvon
was murdered.

Thank goodness, I knew the invisible map of
L.A. like the lines in the palms of my hands. I
learned some of the gang territory from growing up in it, some more of it as an LAPD officer;
then, later, I learned the rest as a private investigator of the hood.

F-Loc had unofficially become part of my
street team, my off-the-record CI—confidential
informant. Each person was like his own little
CIA—central intelligence for the streets.

I gazed up at the pigeons squawking and fill-
ing the sky as I entered the jungle—the place
in L.A. they say has only one way in, and one
way out. The pigeons or tumblers were being
flipped as an announcement of my presence.

Although I hadn't been a policewoman in a couple of years now, the denizens still considered me "one time." This was a game but also an announcement of a potential legal arrival.

The smell of the large Dumpsters wafted in the air. Welcome to the jungle.

I called F-Loc on his private cell phone number as I sat outside his gated apartment building. "Loc."

"What it be?"

"Z, here. I need your help again. I'm out front."

"Let me come down."

Unlike in the past when he was always accompanied by his muscle, F-Loc came down alone. He had learned to trust me over the past two years and never brought his boys with him. He used to bring his bodyguards and frisk me for a wire. He'd learn that I would use information, but his name never got put up in the mix. He trusted that I could get jobs done.

Once he came down, he plopped down in the car seat next to me. I got straight to the point. "My brother's been kidnapped. You know anything about this?"

"Yeah, the streets is buzzin'. Sorry to hear about Mayhem. You know he was always a stand-up dude."

I panicked. "Why are you talking about him in the past tense? Have you heard anything? Is he still alive?"

"No, I don't know. You know these Mexican cartels are beginning to kidnap and take over territory. They pretty ruthless."

"Does that have anything to do with his kidnapping?"

"Naw, but this war on drugs does."

"What do you mean?"

"This war on drugs is a bunch of bullshit. The government don't want to get rid of no drugs. This is an international business. Almost every industry is run through some form of drug money that's been laundered. Rap, the car industry, guns, you name it. Not to mention the crooked cops and the different cartels who ain't gon' get paid if this stuff ever ends."

"So what is your point, F-Loc?"

"It's getting harder and harder for the brothers to make money in L.A. The Feds have cracked down on the border. Business is being conducted out the country now. They've even cracked down on the Colombians."

"And?"

"Word on the street is that a big crime family in Brazil was cutting a deal with Mayhem and this was going to be his new connect. Some of the Eses got mad and felt he was undercutting them. He sent wifey, who used to be one of his mules, to do the deal; plus, she's from Brazil and can speak that Portuguese. Anyhow, she's being held hostage there with the money. Your brother was making some big moves since he got out last year, and somebody didn't like it."

"Do you know anything about his strip club?" My job was like being part of the CIA of the streets. You had to get out there to get information.

"It's cool. I slid through there a few times."

"What's the name of it?"

"The Kitty Kat Koliseum."

"What street is it on?"

"Hollywood Boulevard."

"So it's in Hollywood?"

"Yep."

"How about a tattoo with a snake on a pole?"

"Those could be any of the Mexican gangs, but I think it's mainly part of a family."

"Which tattoo parlor do they use?"

"The main one the Eses use is in the barrio. It's called the Innovative Tattoo Shop."

Someone knocked on my car window on the rider's side and I almost leaped out my skin. It's not always a safe place to be sitting in a car in the jungle.

"F-Loc." I glanced up to see someone who looked like a typical crackhead. Chapped lips. Knotted hair. Dirty. Shaking. "Give me a nickel bag. I swear I'ma pay when I get my GR check first of the month."

"Look, nigga. Do I look like government cheese sittin' up in here? I ain't givin' a nigga a free nothin'. This ain't the welfare. You see me talkin' business. Get yo' ass away from this car before I break my foot off in your ass."

Then, F-Loc turned back to me as if nothing had happened. "Sorry 'bout that. Like I said, shit is dryin' up. I used to could break a nigga off, but not no more. Times is tough out here on the street. I ain't givin' out nothin' but tombstones and ya got to be dead to get those."

I suppressed my laugh, so that he would know I was serious about my business. "Okay, thanks, Loc."

We bumped fists, and he climbed out of my car. Shaking my head, I drove off. I'd worked in the male culture so long as a policewoman, I'd picked up a lot of their ways. That's why I was still trying to detox from all that swearing like the proverbial sailor. It's not ladylike, and whenever I'm around Romero, he treats me like I'm fine china, so now I notice I don't even want to curse.

I didn't know who to believe—F-Loc or the so-called agents. I bet the truth is probably somewhere in the middle.

Chapter Ten

On a hunch, I jumped on the San Bernardino Freeway and drove out to the Innovative Tatto Parlor on Cesar Chavez Avenue. It was when I pulled up in front of the turquoise adobe-looking shop that I decided what I would do. I flashed my badge, quickly, the same way the Feds did to me at the Academy Awards that night.

"Inspector Saldano." I decided to pretend to be an inspector and I spoke with authority. "Who's the owner?"

The shop only had a half dozen patrons in it. Five men and one woman sat in chairs lined up against the wall, waiting patiently, as if they were waiting for a barber. Everyone was speaking Spanish, but I knew the language, which was an advantage. My father taught me Spanish before he died and Chica had taught me a lot of the language when we were growing up together.

Some tattoos were frivolous, but many told a story. I'd read of a case where one man was arrested because he had the murder scene tattooed on his chest, and this scene got him life.

"I am."

"What's your name?"

"Pedro Garcia." A short Hispanic who sat in a stool working on a client looked up and held his drill in midair.

"We had a complaint from the health department."

"Oh, no, senora." I could see the fear in his eyes. I wondered if he even had a business license or whatever was required to have a tattoo parlor. I looked around on the wall and didn't see one on display.

He was working on another Latino man, who had more tattoos on his face than Lil Wayne. "I'd like to see the tools you're using."

He showed me his tattoo gun.

"Do you clean it after each person?"

"*Sí.*"

"We had a complaint from people who had a tattoo that like looks like a snake on a pole. Could you show me a picture of this tattoo?"

He pointed to his wall which had different customers poising with their tattoos. I took a picture of the tattoo with my cell phone.

"I haven't done that one but once. They're common though."

"Do you know who belongs to?"

"It belongs to Bonzo."

I spoke in Spanish. "Do you have an address or phone number for him?"

"No."

"Okay, I'm going to give you a chance to clean this place up. Get your business license, too."

I decided not to press the issue and left. I wrote the name Bonzo down in my cell phone and left. I e-mailed the picture of the tattoo to Chica, who was getting pretty good as a bounty hunter in tracking people down.

Chica called right back. "Where are you, *mija?*" She sounded worried sick. "Are you all right?"

"I decided to try to help my brother."

Chica let out a sigh. "I'm glad you're going to do it, but be careful."

"Did you get the e-mail?"

"*Sí.* What do you want?"

"Do you know which gang sign this tattoo this belongs to?"

"I'm not sure, but I can find out."

"See if you can find a gang member with a street name Bonzo in your database. He would be part of a Mexican gang."

Chica had gotten really good at setting up our own private databases, which I had found to really come in handy as we built our businesses.

"When are you going to go home? Romero even called looking for you. That was a first."

"What do you mean?"

"He sounded a little jealous, too. I'd never heard that in his voice before."

"He had to leave last night on business. I understood. He should understand now that the shoe's on the other foot. Besides, he knows this is the kind of job we both have."

"So you're working?"

"Yes."

"I guess he was just worried because he hadn't heard from you. Keep me posted if you need me."

Chica dropped the subject. She was so happy to be working and standing on her own two feet for the first time in her adult life, she often deferred to my decision. "I appreciate you mentoring me, *mija*. You're really showing me how to work the streets. " She laughed, I guessed recalling her days of prostitution. "I mean, working the streets in a good way. I feel good about myself when I bring in these bail jumpers."

I pulled out my phone and typed down what I could reenact of the abduction.

Chapter Eleven

As I looked over my presumably forged passport, I vacillated between my instinct of fight or flight. I really didn't know what to do. Did I really want to go down this road? These people didn't play. I had no idea what I was going to be going up against. I really didn't want to get involved with his wifey, Appolonia, either, because for one, I didn't know her and, for two, she really wasn't my concern. I guessed she was as my nephews' mother, but I resented that I would have to help her in order to help free my brother. This was a package deal. In order to free my brother, I was going to have to find her to even get the money.

I looked up an Appolonia Silva, and I couldn't find any record for her online. I also checked databases that I'd learned how to hack from Okamoto, who was a geek/hacker. I tried the Department of Motor Vehicles and checked the Department of Justice databases. I wondered if she was in the country illegally. The Appolonia Silva I did find only had a record in the last twelve years. Before that, her life seemed murky. She was like a female Adam. Just appeared on earth. At least Eve was taken from Adam's rib.

I went online with my phone and looked up Rio de Janeiro, Brazil. Before I could get into the politics, the war on drug problem, the rainforest, my phone rang. I glanced down. It was Romero.

"Where are you?" His voice sounded like controlled anger. At the same time, it cracked with anxiety. I'd never heard him that upset. "Are you okay? Where have you been?"

"You wouldn't believe what has happened." I couldn't even muster up the courage to tell him what I'd been through.

"Yes, I had a bad night too, but when I got back home I expected to find you here. You all right?"

"I left you a message. I've been working all night too. How about if I come by there after I go to the doctor?"

"What doctor? Are you okay?"

"Long story. I can't tell you."

"When are you ever going to trust me?" Romero implored.

I changed the subject. "Did you settle your case?"

"Not quite. Just some leads we had to follow up. We've busted a big methamphetamine lab in a white collar neighborhood. We got a lot of suspects in custody. Be surprised the people committing crimes these days. But y'know with plea bargaining how things are."

"Yeah, that's true. Even Orange County is having a series of bank robberies committed by white dudes. People are desperate with this unemployment. Well, I'll be over there."

"Say no more. I'll have the tub ready when you get here."

I passed Pink's, the famous hot dog stand in Hollywood near Melrose, and stopped and picked up a chili dog. The hot dog stand was on my way to the doctor's office, which was located near Westwood. The doctor, who was supposed to be an epidemiologist of sorts, seemed a little shady, but judging from all the actors' pictures on his wall, everyone uses these types of doctors to get out of work and on sick leaves to pursue their acting dreams. After getting inoculated with my ten-year tetanus shot and yellow fever shots, I got the prescription for Lariam.

An hour later, I picked up the prescription, then drove to Silver Lake to see Romero. I didn't want to tell him anything. I just wanted to fall into the flannel warmth of his embrace. Within his arms, I always felt comfort. Maybe I could feel normal again, a sense of safety.

When I arrived, I found Romero asleep on his sofa. His mouth was wide open and he sounded like he was sawing logs his snores were so loud. "Poor baby," I whispered, kissing his forehead.

To keep from waking Romero, I tiptoed to the bathroom. He had already run my bubble bath and the water was sitting in his old-fashioned tub with the lion claw feet. I tested the water with my index finger, and it had grown cool. I let some of the tepid water out, then put in fresh hot water. I climbed in the tub and before I knew it I was out like a light.

I woke up to Romero gently soaping my back, and I smiled. I was surprised at how much time had passed. I could see through his bathroom window that it was dark outside.

"You were zonked out, *mamacita*. Bad case?"

I nodded. "Wound up working all night."

"Me, too." I could see Romero's five o'clock shadow. I guessed he hadn't slept until he dropped down for his nap on his sofa. He usually stayed clean shaven.

My mind was on my brother and I wasn't really feeling the lovemaking like I usually would. My mind kept spinning as Romero kissed me up in bed.

"What's wrong, baby? Not in the mood?" he asked, raising his torso from between my legs and scooting over. I could tell he was disappointed, but he was not the type to push the issue.

I shook my head. My mind was spinning. I was torn. Should I tell him about my brother's kidnapping? How could I tell him I was going to go out the country? I guess Romero sensed my withdrawal and he just scooted behind me, spooning me, his arms wrapped around my waist. I fell asleep, and so did he. We'd both had a long night.

It was after ten-thirty when I woke up. I jack-knifed up, determined to make my escape. I wanted to get back out to the street before I left the country.

I slid out from under Romero's arm and leg he had thrown over me. He must have already been awake, because he grabbed my left hand as soon as I placed one foot on the floorboard. He didn't say anything, but in his touch I felt his strong need and desire. I paused. I wanted him, but I also wanted to see if I could find out any leads on my brother's kidnapping. Feeling conflicted, I thought about what Shirley had said. *Listen to your heart.*

Suddenly it hit me. I didn't know when I'd hold my man in my arms again. Without giving it another thought, I slid back under the covers.

I laced my fingers into Romero's, then climbed on top of him and began deep kissing him. I loved to kiss Romero because it always reminded me of our first kiss at a Starbucks and because he was such a good kisser. His hands slid up and down my body, and I just surrendered to the moment. I didn't want to think. I didn't want to worry about my problems. I just wanted to feel and enjoy the golden pleasure my man was giving me.

"Are you sure?" he asked, referring to the fact he didn't have on a condom. "Do you want me to pull out?"

I don't know what I was thinking; my mind was a blank and I didn't answer. My periods were irregular, so I assumed I wasn't that fertile. I was thirty-five and had never been pregnant before. I generally took birth control pills, and used condoms, but I'd gotten relaxed with Romero and only used the condoms. Plus, our relationship was exclusive. How did I know? When Romero wasn't at work, or with his daughter, he was with me, and vice versa. Totally the opposite of the one I'd had with the late undercover cop, whoremonger Flag.

I continued riding on a crest, a hot wave sweeping into my belly. All I knew was I had to leave my man satisfied. I felt like I was on a magical sea, being buoyed and tossed about by a wave. I was drowning in such sweet pleasure, nothing seemed to bother me. I had only intended to satisfy Romero, not myself. It was going to be a testament to all the kindness he'd shown me, to all the good times we'd had over the past year. I wanted to thank him with my body and soul for showing me that love was still a possibility.

Instead of my just pleasing Romero, as the pressure mounted, I exploded in cauldron of sheer ecstasy myself. I wound up crying and screaming out his name at the same time of our mutual orgasms. Afterward, I clung to him, my toes curling up, as if he were the Holy Grail. I burst into tears.

"I love you, *mamí*," Romero said, kissing my lips, then my shoulder as we both panted, spent. He kissed my tears as they rolled down my face. "Baby, I'm sorry I didn't pull out. I'm so sorry. You just felt so good. I couldn't . . ."

"Shush." I put my finger to his lips. I wasn't worried about anything. "I don't even know why I'm crying. I just thought of what my life would be like without you."

I continued crying into Romero's shoulder and he patted my shoulder. "It's okay, *mamacita*. Everything is going to be okay."

I felt like I was drowning and these would be my last words. I tried to imagine my life without Romero and it made me sob even more.

When I met him, I didn't believe love even existed anymore. Now I knew what it was like to see the light shine on a man's shoulder and know love. I knew what early spring flowers looked like when you saw them through the prism of love.

I loved the way Romero loved his daughter, Bianca, from his first marriage. I loved how he was born poor in El Barrio, was part of a crime family, but refused to let that define him. I loved the way he left his leader status as a gang member behind when he was young and put himself through college. I loved how he was a straight cop, who was liked by his peers and even respected by a lot of the hoods on the street.

Romero was the first man who pointed out the Big Dipper to me. I didn't know when I first knew I loved him, but he always said he loved me from the first time he met me, during the L.A. riots, when he rescued me from a hostage situation. For the first time, I answered, "I love you, Romero."

Romero kissed me passionately in return. "I know I once said I'd never do this again, but Z"—he paused—"will you marry me?" He reached under the pillow.

I was shocked. "What did you say?" I couldn't believe my ears.

"Will you marry me?"

I let out an "ahh" breath as if I'd been hit in my solar plexus. Finally, I spoke up. "Baby, it's too soon." I didn't say anything, but I liked how things were between us. Comfortable, warm,

and happy. Why did he have to go ruin everything with this marriage talk? I told him I was
not marriage material. My previous marriage
and annulment had been hell.

"Soon?" Romero protested. "I've loved you
since the first time I saw you, standing up to
those three thugs, like, 'Hey, bring it on.' I
knew back then there was something special
about you. Since we hooked back up, you've
been more than I could imagine. I'm so proud
of the way you've rebuilt your life and remained
sober. I saw you go through hell last year after
Trayvon's death and yet you landed on your
feet. You're a good friend to me and to others.
You're a good detective. A good lover.

"When you're in something, you'll see it
through all the way. I've seen you put your life
on the line for your dead nephew. I just love
how you love with all your heart and soul. And
I'd be proud to have you as my wife."

"Wow!" I didn't see this coming.

"Reach under the pillow, babe," Romero said.

I reached under the pillow and searched until my fingers felt a box. Puzzled, I opened the
box. Inside was a beautiful platinum Marquise
diamond ring.

I gasped. "Oh, Romero, you shouldn't have."

"Is that a yes or a no?"

I heaved a deep sigh. I couldn't answer him, I
was so overcome. I said a resounding yes in my
heart, but I couldn't commit now. Now I was
even more conflicted since I had this issue to
deal with my brother.

"I'll keep the ring on the dresser for you. It's your call."

"Let's just go back to sleep," I said, pulling the duvet covers up over us. Romero wrapped his arms around me and snuggled up. I lay still and listened to his breath until I felt him dozing off into sleep. Afterward, I untangled my limbs from his, then took a quick shower. I found a dressy black leather pants set and tall boots which folded at the knees that I'd left at his house and slipped into them. I was on a mission. If I didn't get away from the comfort of Romero's love, I'd never be able to go through with what I had to do. I grabbed my purse, which had my Glock in it.

Romero's eyes flew open just as I tried to creep past his bed. "Where are you going, *mija?*"

I paused. "I've got to leave, baby."

"Why?"

"I can't tell you. This is family business."

"Sure you've got to go? Why don't you spend the night?"

"I've got to go." I was insistent.

"We've gotten so close. Don't you trust me?"

"I don't know who to trust anymore."

"That's cold. Didn't you just tell me you loved me?"

"I meant it."

"Well, tell me something."

"Shoot."

"We've been together over a year and you still don't trust me?"

"Talking about trust. Do you ever tell me about that family of yours?"

"I told you that's my past."

"What is the name of your family's gang?"

"Out of family loyalty, I can't tell you."

I thought about his crime family. Were they a part of Mayhem's kidnapping? What was his family's name? It really didn't matter. All I cared about was whether they were the ones who had Mayhem. Would blood be thicker than mud, in this case? I didn't know. But one thing I knew for sure. I had to do this by myself.

Chapter Twelve

I hated to part on bad terms with Romero. We seldom fought or even disagreed. We gave each other our space and our freedom to work our individual cases and it seemed to work for us. But now he was talking about marriage. He was serious, but I had doubts. Would a marriage end our happy relationship?

It was after midnight as I drove through the underbelly of Hollywood where Mayhem's strip club called the Kitty Kat Koliseum was located. I decided I need to snoop around and see if anyone knew anything. I really didn't exactly know what I was looking for. I parked my car a block away and strode past the hookers of all races strolling the Hollywood strip to enter into the more legal form of prostitution. Walking the streets or having sex with a lap dance partner—what was the difference?

I could hear the beat of the music from the outside. Even the ground was vibrating because the noise was so loud. I was surprised to see a line at this time of morning, but there was one. Once I got inside, I scanned the room. The club was not what I expected. It was decorated like a Roman coliseum with different levels of sofas in a circle. A stage was nestled in the center.

I put the trip to Brazil in the back of my mind. If I could find Mayhem, then I wouldn't even have to go out the country, was what I was reasoning. But, they still wanted the money and planned to kill him without it. Also, his wifey was the one who had access to the money. She was in Brazil and I was going to have to go there to find her. So backing out was not going to be an option.

Just considering the complexity of my case, for a fleeting moment, I thought about ordering a drink, but then I decided to get a 7 Up.

I didn't know the bartender, the bouncer, or the lead dancer, but I decided I needed to talk to them. They would be a good place to start as sources of information. They may have had information or not, but it was worth a shot. I started with the bartender. I just had to make him feel important.

Even if I found out where Mayhem was, how could I get him released without the money? I just wanted to find out if there was anything I could do before I caught a plane to Brazil. I hadn't flown since 9/11. I still had nightmares about those two planes going into the two Trade Center buildings. To say I had a fear of flying would be an understatement.

I adjusted my eyes to the blue strobe nightlights, and for a moment, I used my hands as binoculars. Tonight the club was packed with thugs, gangsters, Crips, and wannabes. I thought I even saw a Compton rapper. I observed several local rapper groups, Revelations, Hitch, and Apocalypse, and the groupies were out six deep to a man.

The room was overflowing with women who could be poster children for steatopygia or the "big butt club." Broke or not, from the looks of things, most of these dancers had gone out and bought big booty transplants. Now you can't tell me everybody had back like this before. Second to the butt transplants were breast implants, but they didn't seem as prominent in this strip club. The trend had changed and now big bottoms were in style.

The place reeked of cigarette smoke, chronic, alcohol, cheap perfume, fish, and unwashed behind. Obviously, strip joints were still an ongoing diversion for men—in spite of the recession. Money was still available for sex and fantasies.

I weaved my way through the crowd of lounging men at tables, making "it rain," as they tossed dollar bills on the stage. Women wearing thongs and bikini tops, giving lap dances, doing booty pops, and clapping their cheeks swarmed around the club or sat with clients.

My purpose was to talk to the bartender, so I made a beeline for the bar. Bartenders were like street corner psychiatrists. They knew everybody's business. Who ran the club in Mayhem's absence was what I wanted to know. Everything seemed like business as usual, and it was what appeared to be a lucrative business.

As I approached the bar, my hands began to tremble. Being in this bar setting was by no means an easy feat for me. Like many newly recovering alcoholics, it was almost a knee-jerk reaction for me to want to take a drink. In spite of all the trouble that alcohol caused me in the past, for a fleeting moment, I entertained the idea of a drink. Yes, I just wanted one drink.

My palate watered like Pavlov's dog just being near the bar, and I could already taste a cool beer guzzling down my throat. Let me be honest about something. I loved how alcohol smelled, and how it tasted. I also liked how I felt when I took that first drink. Unfortunately, that one drink was never enough for me, and it had derailed my career as a police.

I hadn't been to my AA meetings in over twenty-four hours and I was already getting tempted. I had to stop walking toward the bar and catch a hold of myself. Just for a mental refresher's course, just in case, in a lapse of sanity, I had to be brutal with myself.

Just in case I wanted to entertain any illusions I could handle a drink again, I had to mentally shake myself up. Even if I wanted to delude myself into thinking I could afford to slip and take just an itsy-bitsy thimble of alcohol, I needed to kick myself in my own butt. I treaded my mind back down memory lane.

What I saw was an ugly picture. The black-outs, the hangovers, the vomiting, the hot-boxes, the detox, the shame, and the degradation. I reminded myself of these past two years of struggle to remain sober, one day at a time, and, once again, I knew I could not afford to give in to that momentary pleasure. I could never get lulled into a false sense of security and think I was cured. There was no cure for alcoholism.

I didn't want to lose two years of hard-won sobriety so I repeated my mantra. *I cannot take a drink. I cannot take a drink. I will remain sober, one day at a time.*

As I got closer, I noticed the bartender wore a name tag on his pink shirt. He was a ripped, muscular dude but was very effeminate acting. He also had great interpersonal skills and was warm with all the customers. "Hey, honey," he called out to men and women alike.

"Hey, Tyrone. What'chu know good?"

"It's all good."

I said a quick prayer, and the moment for lusting after a drink passed. I sighed in relief. I decided to just focus on the matter on hand. Who had taken Mayhem? Did his business associates have anything to do with his disappearance?

Resolutely, I ordered a 7 Up. "Hello, Tyrone. My name is Z. I'm David's—I mean, Mayhem's—sister. Have you seen him?" I smiled, and shook his hand.

He started looking uncomfortable. "No, but you might ask the manager. He's been looking for him."

"Where is he?"

"There he go over there." He pointed with his eyes slanted in a flat line. My eyes followed over to the VIP area. The area was raised high above the rest of the club, and was cordoned off with a golden braided rope. The person in question was a tall brother with cornrows who wore shades that had reflective mirrors in them. He was dressed in an expensive white Armani suit, which glistened under the nightlights.

"What's his name?"

"G-Man."

"Could you let him know that I'd like to talk to him?" I paused. "It's important." I stopped Tyrone as he reached for his cell. "Before you call him, can you tell me who the bouncer is?"

"Name's Bone. He's over by the door."

Other than on a few cases when I was a cop, I'd never frequented a strip joint. I guess it's a man thing. I really don't like how the women are being objectified as sex toys, but I try not to judge. Many people were doing what they had to do in this economy. I reflected on a recent newscast where women who used to be professionals in corporate America had turned to stripping to help take care of their families. I guess it wasn't any different than housewives in Beverly Hills using the pole in their bedrooms to spice up their sex lives and hold on to their Hollywood executive husbands.

The whole world was frozen in upside down mold. Houses were under water with upside down mortgages and people were drowning with upside down lives.

Tyrone called G-Man and I watched him pick up his cell and answer. I stood waiting, since I assumed he would have to handle the business he had at hand. There were several more customers with him.

I watched G-Man nod, saying it was okay for me to go over to him. "You can see him now." He acted like he was some big-time CEO.

From where I was sitting on the barstool, the first thing I sized up and didn't like was how

G-Man was acting like he was "the man" now. He was sitting in the VIP area, toking on an un-lit cigar, and flossing his loud flashy platinum rings and chains. He had two girls sitting on both knees. He was a portly man with an enor-mous prognathous jaw, but he was carrying on like the late Biggie Smalls. Like his money and power made him the finest thing out there among the pretty young girls.

I decided to find out all I could from him.

The strippers on his lap looked like JB, jail bait, underage, and this really turned me off with him, but I had to think about my brother. He slapped the girls on their behinds, and they got up, sashaying off.

"I'm Z, David's—I mean, Big Homie aka May-hem's sister."

"Yeah, he told me about you. Use to be 5-0. Sure you not with them anymore?"

"No, I'm not with LAPD anymore. I'd like to ask you a few questions. When was the last time you saw Big Homie?"

I watched his eye flinch, just ever so slightly, in the corner, and I knew he was lying before he spoke, but I just registered this information in the back of my head. *Suspicious behavior.* "I saw him three days ago. Yeah, that's right. He hasn't been by here in about three days."

"Is that normal?"

"Generally, he comes through on the week-end, checking on things. Picking up money. Overseeing payroll. I have some business to talk to him about."

"Have you heard from him?" I paused. I really didn't expect him to tell the truth.

"No. Why?"

I thought about it. If G-Man was involved, if he'd sold Mayhem out, there was no sense in asking for his support. I would deal with him later. I didn't answer. I flashed the picture on my cell phone. "Have you seen someone with a tattoo like this?"

"There're a lot like that. They're part of a gang sign. Sort of like the medical sign. A snake wrapped around a pole."

"Do you know any of the patrons who might have one?"

"Bonzo has one like that."

"Who is Bonzo?

"He hangs around here and one of your brother's massage parlors, Soft Touch. He comes through here a lot."

"Is he here tonight?"

"I saw him earlier, but it's crowded now, so I don't see him."

"What does he look like?"

"Mexican." He stretched his hand out flat, perpendicular to his chest. "He's about yay high. Wears a ponytail. Kind of medium height."

"How about the lead dancer? Can I talk to her?"

"Oh, our bottom bitch?"

I looked at him, throwing him some shade, and smirked. He got my drift that I didn't care for him disrespecting women. I guess he saw my distaste for the word and he corrected himself. "Yes, that's Chutney. That's her performing now, but you can talk to her when she gets through."

The current dance was performed by a svelte woman on stage dressed in a gold and white sheer Cleopatra outfit. She wore a shoulder-length wig with bangs, accompanied by dark eye kohl. She did a slow strip tease down to a pearl belted chain and G-string. She gracefully danced her way around the stage, did a deep split and waltzed back up, until she pirouetted over to the pole. She spun around the pole, never missing a beat, and turned upside down.

T.I.'s "I'm Flexing" was playing in the background. There was something different about this stripper. She moved sensuously and suggestively like a professional modern dancer. Probably just another girl who came to Hollywood with stardom in her eyes and wound up on the pole.

"Can I talk to Chutney?"

He nodded. When Chutney pranced over with grace in her tall stilettos, he introduced us.

"You're very talented," I commented as she eased down into the chair next to me.

Chutney was fanning her face to cool off. "I've danced in a few videos." She flashed a fake modest, yet demure, smile. Her high cheekbones shone with pride.

G-Man introduced me, and stepped away. "This Big Homie's sister."

Chutney's eyes lit up, just a tad bit too much. "Oh, my goodness! You're his baby sister, Z." She reached out and gave me a hug. "He always brags on you. Say you's a bad bitch. I read the paper where you took down two dirty narcs by yourself. "

I ignored her remark. I didn't like how women had embraced the word bitch, and I didn't like how, when you stood up for yourself as a woman, you were called this name. "When did you see him last?"

"It's been a minute. I think he came through here last weekend."

"I need to ask you something personal."

Tears flooded her eyes. Right away, I could tell there was more to this relationship than business. She was definitely Mayhem's woman. I could see it all in her eyes and it was written all over her face.

"Was your relationship more than business?"

She hesitated before she spoke. Her lips trembled, and she bit the bottom one and nodded. "We done broke up now though. That mulatto-looking heffa, Appolonia, found out and came down here and raised hell a few weeks ago. David cut me off"—she snapped her fingers—"just like that. I never thought he was that pussy whipped. Just because she one o' his babies' mamas and 'cause she raisin' them other two kids, that don't make her his wife. She just wifey."

I didn't say anything. Now I was getting curious about this wifey, Appolonia.

"You don't understand. I love David. That gold-digging bitch don't love him like I do."

Something inside told me Chutney didn't know anything about my brother's disappearance and I didn't press the issue, either. So

Mayhem had an outside woman, but I wasn't that surprised. Drug dealers possessed rock star celebrity status in the ghetto.

I finished the evening talking to the bouncer, Bone, but I couldn't pick up any information from him. He was the muscle at the club, but he wasn't too informative. I could see why they called him Bone, because he was truly a bonehead.

I decided to try the massage parlor next.

Chapter Thirteen

I drove over to the massage parlor, not knowing what I would find. The first thing that surprised me was what looked like a crew of cameramen. They were pushing high-definition digital camera equipment and looked like the crews I would see on the streets whenever a Hollywood movie studio was shooting a film on location in L.A.

"What are you doing here?" I asked a man standing nearby the door. He ignored me. Then I noticed a former police officer I used to work with named Officer Leonard Jackson. I gave him a knowing look. Jackson gave me a sheepish grin. I could tell the way he was dressed that he was not on a security job, but on a pornography job. He was wearing suspenders with a pair of tight Speedo pants.

"Hey, Jackson, is it?" I asked. "What are you doing here?"

"What are you doing here?" He answered a question with a question. He slid his hand over his bald head in a nervous gesture.

"I'm here as part of an investigation." I flashed my ID and I could see his eyes almost jet out his head, almost cartoon-like. "Who is the manager?"

He stammered when he spoke. "That's Mr. Dickinson, but he's not here at night."

"Well, who is the night supervisor?"

"His name is Lester."

"Where is he?"

"He's down the hall." He pointed down a corridor.

"So are you working here?" I probed.

"Sort of," he mumbled.

"You still with the department?"

"Yes." Then he thought of a way to try to back me off. He didn't want me to know he was a porn star during his down time from the police department. "I heard what happened to your partner and what happened with you. I'm sorry to hear about it."

I wasn't sure if he was talking about my getting fired or my getting shot in the line of duty. I studied him and realized he was referring to me being fired. The old me would have been too ashamed or embarrassed to talk about it. He wasn't going to be able to back me down with that one. I was no longer ashamed.

Not one to be deterred, I didn't let it floor me. "Well, it's all good. I've developed a second career from that tragedy, so not everything is a curse. I'm here tonight because of a case I'm working on."

He nodded.

"So they shoot pornography here?" I shot from the hip. I pointed at the cameras, which went behind closed doors.

Jackson didn't answer. He just rushed into a back room and closed the door.

I walked down the hallway and noticed most of the doors were closed where patrons were supposedly getting massages. I could smell incense and scented candles. Soft music played over the intercom.

I tapped on a back door to Lester's office.

"Come in," a voice called out.

I opened the door into what looked like a typical corporate office. Lester was working on a computer. He swiveled around in his chair.

"Hello, my name is Zipporah Saldano. I'm here regarding my brother, Mayhem—I mean, David. I understand he owns this place."

Lester, a slightly built man, jumped to his feet and held out his hand. "Yes, how may I help you?"

"Have you seen my brother?"

"No. I was looking for him earlier today. Generally he comes through on the weekend."

"When did you last talk to him?"

"I talked to him Monday or Tuesday. We were going over the books. Why? Is everything all right?"

"Yes. He's fine." I decided not to alarm him. I got the vibe that he didn't have anything to do with Mayhem's kidnapping and he didn't know anything. "If you hear from him, have him contact me."

Lester gave me his business card, and I left.

Chapter Fourteen

After I left the massage parlor, I felt down-hearted and discouraged. I really hadn't learned anything there, other than it could easily be a modern brothel, a house of pornography, and it was scheduled to close at 2:00 A.M. I could tell how each room was closed that this was a private dance between the client and the female masseuses.

I had to get out of L.A. and it was almost two in the morning. Time was running out. My plane was scheduled to leave in the early afternoon. Since 9/11, you had to be at LAX at least two hours early. And I still needed to go by the office and then get home and pack. Even though G-Man didn't admit to knowing that my brother had been kidnapped, I felt he was hiding something. He was acting innocent, but inside, I felt he had motive to sell Mayhem out. I wouldn't put anything past him, now that he was acting like Big Willie.

As I was trying to get to my car, so I could drive to my office in Santa Monica and get home to pack, I thought I heard footsteps. I sensed someone was following me, but I wasn't sure. I stopped walking. The sound stopped. I eased my piece out my slingshot and let it drop down to my side.

Whenever I stopped walking, the sound would stop. I looked around me and for the first time noticed that the street was dark. The streetlight was at the far end of the street. Why had I parked so far away? I wondered. Then I remembered. I had parked down the street because the parking lot had been full when I arrived.

I decided to pretend I was unaware of anyone following me. Step. Step. Step. Stop. I swallowed a lump in my throat. Once again the shushing sound stopped. A susurrus sound in the tree branches whooshed overhead. I could smell alcohol in the air. Whoever it was following me had been drinking.

I clicked my car door opener, and that's when my stalker attacked. Whoever he or she was jumped me and attacked from behind. Even though I thought I was prepared, my assailant still caught me by surprise. I dropped my gun in the tussle.

Whoever it was seemed to be as tall as me because I was able to fling him off, and toss him over my shoulder. I did a long-legged kick from tae kwon do. I grabbed the person, who turned out to be a man, and cold cocked him in a barrage of punches. I picked up my gun and pulled it on him. In a swift move, I disarmed him of his gun. In the dark, I could tell it was a Latino guy.

"Stop, stop!" He held up both hands in surrender and locked his body into a fetal position.

"What do you want? Who sent you to kill me?" I demanded.

"I wasn't going to kill you. I was just supposed to shake you up. Scare you off."

"I'm going to ask one more time. Who sent you? Otherwise I'll put this bullet right between your eyes." I cocked my gun and held it between his eyes.

"I'm one of Bonzo's boys. He heard you been asking about him. He just wanted me to shake you up."

"What's your name?"

"Jorge." He pronounced it "Hor-hay."

"Where is my brother? Do you know who has Mayhem?" I balled up my fist and started to sock him again.

"I swear on my mother's grave, I know nothing."

I held my gun to his face and pressed it by his nose. "Tell Bonzo if anyone harms my brother, I'll come after them. Now *get!*"

I watched Jorge run off into the darkness without his gun. I let out a deep breath and tried to gather my composure. Feeling paranoid, I picked up Jorge's gun, then climbed in my car.

Chapter Fifteen

Still feeling discombobulated, I drove off from the massage parlor aka house of prostitution. For all of its front, it was still a brothel. I could still smell the candles and the incense used as aromatherapy. I could tell more was going on than massages, but that wasn't my concern. My concern was the attack on me. Obviously, someone was following me. Who had already gotten on to the fact I was out seeking answers?

After this surprise attack, I almost changed my mind about going to my Santa Monica office. I reprimanded myself as I drove. "You're in enemy territory."

"Be careful," I whispered out loud to myself. I didn't flip on the radio because I wanted to be alert to any more attacks. I was behind enemy lines and the next time I'd have to disguise myself better. Just to be on the safe side, I kept my gun on the seat. I wiped my prints off Jorge's gun and dropped it down a drain near Venice. Maybe it wasn't worth it to do any more snooping. I needed to get ready to get out of town and do what I need to do without further mishap. I decided to go to the office, but I had to tie up loose ends. For one, I had to cancel the contract with the missing starlet Lolita's family. I needed to mail back their check. I also wanted to see if I could see who the owners were on papers of the Kitty Kat Koliseum and the Soft Touch Massage Parlor.

What else would I find out? I knew Mayhem was an entrepreneur. So now I knew he didn't make all his money from drug money. What was that the Feds said about him selling illegal cell phones in prison? I thought about Tank's mention of his Internet businesses and my brother trying to get into producing rap. He was more multi-dimensional than I would have ever guessed.

I'd never known about his massage parlor or the strip joint. I wondered whose name they were under.

I wouldn't have time to follow up on Bonzo before I left, but I'd deal with that later. As I drove, I kept checking my rearview mirror, which was a habit for me these days. Last year while I was tracking down Trayvon's murderer, I was often being followed by the same murderers, so now I always took that precaution. I always checked my back seat before I climbed into my car, whether day or night, too.

I headed back to our office in Santa Monica since I needed to tie up loose ends before going out of the country. Our office had large diagonal marble tiles on the floor, a fancy Louis XVI antique sofa in the waiting room. We each had our own cubicles in the back with our individual computers. Ficus plants decorated the room for the green effect.

I pulled out the cards of the two agents who'd pulled me in and looked them up online. They both sounded legit. I e-mailed Lolita's family and let them know I would not be able to follow up on the case. I reimbursed them $2,000 on PayPal. I looked up Rio de Janeiro and the surrounding favelas and found there was a civil war on drugs going on at that moment where the government was trying to clean up the city. There was a travel advisory, but what could I do? I went on YouTube and saw interviews with the traffickers who had their heads covered with knit ski masks.

I thought about Romero's proposal and decided I'd think about that later. I had too much on my plate.

I held my head in my hands. I was tired and needed to just shut my eyes. What was I getting into?

I dozed off into a fitful sleep. I dreamed about my father, who'd been dead over twenty years. He always came to me in my sleep whenever I was faced with a lot of problems. In this dream, I was a little girl and my father was taking me to his new house he'd just purchased in Compton. I loved this stucco bungalow complete with the little picket fence, the American Dream, and everything was perfect except for one thing.

This was the first time I met his new wife, Ernestine. I could tell, even in my dream, that she didn't like me. She had her own little boy, Dre, who was the same age as me at the time (seven), and she didn't like how my father paid so much attention to me.

I guessed I was spending the weekend. Later that night, my father and Ernestine argued over how much attention he paid to me. I overheard her say, "She's going to turn out like her no-good mother anyway. An apple doesn't fall far from its tree."

What my father said would shape my path for the rest of my life. "Well, this my seed and she's gonna to be something special."

In my dream, I heard the doorbell ringing, then a rapping at the office door, and I woke up with a warm feeling. My daddy had said I was special. The words every little girl needed when they were growing up. Probably made a difference in why I wasn't dancing on the pole down to this day. Not that I'm knocking it; I'm just glad it's not my thing.

At first I looked around. Disoriented, I had to think for a moment. Where was I? Then I remembered I had stopped by the office and had fallen asleep on the sofa.

I jumped up to answer the door, thinking it was UPS or FedEx. All the time my mind was on how I needed to get home and get ready for my plane trip. I was wondering who was coming by the office this early in the morning. I glanced at our digital clock and saw it was seven in the morning. I opened the door, my gun behind my back, cocked and ready to be drawn, but no one was there. I glanced up and down the street. Hmmm. The street was empty. In our office district, there were no cars in the parking lot yet. I was getting ready to turn away, when I glanced down and was surprised to see what

looked like a wicker basket on the single plat-
form step outside our office.

Without a thought, I opened the basket,
thinking maybe it was mistakenly left behind on the doorstep. Truth be known, I really wasn't thinking of anything as I lifted the
lid. My first reaction was one of shock. I felt
strangely disembodied. I was in that primitive
place where there once was no language, no
words. I couldn't even think of a word to de-
scribe what my primal reaction was.

Then, in the second between what I observed
and what hit my brain synapses registered, I
recoiled in disbelief and let out a bloodcurdling
scream. I'm not the type of female to faint, but
if I were, I would have passed out. This was
too much. The first thing I recognized was the
short fade haircut. Then I recognized the face.
It was Tank's face. There was a puddle of blood
beginning to coagulate at the neckline. Someone had beheaded Tank like John the Baptist!
For a moment, I stood transfixed in horror.

"Oh, my God! Tank, what have they done to
you?" I hollered. I wondered where his body
was. "Who did this to you?" I knew it was use-
less talking out loud to a dead person, but I had
to say something. I knew this was a warning.

Tank's eyes were wide open so I was sure he
was conscious when this barbarian cut off his
head. I shook my head. Now I was really getting afraid. What the hell was I getting into?
This shit was sick! I needed to back out of this
mess. I couldn't go on like this. I wasn't up for
getting my head cut off. What kind of bullshit

was this anyway? Now if I ever needed a drink this was the time.

I guess that's when I saw the envelope. I opened it. There was a note inside which read:

This will be your brother next, so get moving! You have one week from today to get that money back.

I mulled over this for a moment. My mind went blank. I couldn't do anything but sit down at my desk, head resting on my fists, just like I was stumped over a banking problem or something like that, and tried to figure out what to do next. Who could I call? I thought of Romero but I hadn't included him in my plan to go out the country and it would involve too much explaining. Plus, he was a by-the-book officer and he'd call his supervisor, and I'd never get out of L.A. I hadn't shared what was going on in the first place and he was always trying to get me to open up. He would be mad about that.

So I scratched Romero's name off the mental list. Next, I thought about calling Chica, but if she got caught with this head in a basket and she already had a criminal record with two strikes, she could wind up back in prison for life.

Now I had a new dilemma. What could I do with Tank's head where it wouldn't be traced back to me? It was not that I was guilty, but I knew how the law worked. The person who reported a vic was generally the first suspect.

No, I had to get out the country and I didn't have time to give a police report. I steeled myself to do what I had to do. I knew I had to go on. I called F-Loc and left him a cryptic message.

"Loc, I'm going underground. I'll get back with you." He understood that meant I needed him to be my ears and eyes in my absence.

I put the basket in my car's front seat and prayed the police didn't pull me over. How could I ever explain this one? I drove to the ocean in Santa Monica and left the basket out in the opening near the jogging trail. I made sure there were no cameras around. Big Brother is always watching you now.

Afterward, I went to a phone booth, which was difficult to find, then called 911 and dropped an anonymous tip. I disguised my voice. "The victim can be found at Santa Monica Pier." I wiped my prints when I left.

I went home and packed my clothes. I called Chica and told her to come get Ben and keep him for me.

"*Mija,* you know I would, but we can't keep pets in our apartment. Besides Riley is allergic to pets. Call Haviland. She's got that big house. And she's been waiting to hear from you anyway."

As much as I hated to call Haviland, the drama queen, I did. My back was up against the wall. I needed her help.

"Chick, where have you been?" Haviland exploded. "We started to call the popo. Why didn't you call us?"

I almost laughed since Haviland sounded funny when she tried to talk "hood." "So who put you on the Z Patrol Unit?" I quipped. "Slow your roll. Calm down. I'm okay."

She backed up then. "Well, you could've called us." Peeved, she decided to try to "guilt" me. "You go to the Oscars with us and then you just disappear like that. We were worried about you."

I ignored her remark. "Did anyone we know win?" I was referring to the picture that Trevor had a small role in.

"No, but it has still been good PR. He's already gotten two new scripts to look at from his agent."

"Great!" Then I went straight to the point. "I need a favor."

"Shoot."

"Can you keep Ben? I've got to go out the country. It's serious business."

"Oh, hell no. Not Ben—that rat." Haviland sounded adamant.

"Look, that rat—and he's not a rat, he's a ferret—saved my life. I really will owe you one if you can do this for me."

Haviland paused, then she pretended to confer with Trevor, as if she were a submissive wife or partner. I guessed she'd been watching how me and Chica acted around our men. "Hon, can we keep Z's pet, Ben?"

Trevor grabbed the phone, happy to be included in the conversation. His voice almost sounded jovial, to know I was involving him in my business. "Z, sure. When do you plan to drop him off?"

"I won't have time to drop him off. You can ask Shirley to let you in my apartment and get him and his cage. Make sure you get his food too. You can go online and look up how to take care of a ferret. You've got to let him out every day to play. He likes to hide under things, so you'll have to be careful. Don't lose him."

Chapter Sixteen

I packed in a hurry, surprised I even had the presence of mind to go through such a menial chore as packing after what I'd just seen. I kept seeing an image of Tank's head in my mind. My hands were shaking like they used to do when I needed a drink, but that was the furthest thing from my mind. I was just spooked. I didn't even know who I was anymore. What kind of person was I to dispose of a head in the park? Then, in the next breath, I rationalized my actions. I was under pressure and I had to get out the country.

On the one hand, I felt guilty like a hit and run driver, but, on the other, time was of the essence. Tank was already dead, I reasoned. There was no sense in losing my brother too. I was under pressure and I did what I had to do.

Somehow, I managed to throw several pair of jeans, underwear, an all-occasion black dress, and jacket with my toothbrush into a small roller bag. I looked at my bookshelf and grabbed Sun Tzu's *The Art of War,* my Blue Book, The Alcoholic Anonymous Bible, and my *King James Bible*, which I put in my carry-on bag. I went to my bank and bought $5,000 in

Traveler's Checks. I decided I'd worry about getting paid from Mayhem later, if there was going to be a later.

I headed to LAX from Baldwin Hills and made it in record time. I left my car in overnight parking. I managed to get through the checkpoint at the airport with no problem, but I had to check my gun, even though it was licensed and registered. Now I really felt vulnerable. I hoped I'd be able to get one once I got to Rio.

I did look up the anonymous account on the flash drive. It was an account in the Cayman Islands. The password and account number was there and this account had over $1 billion in it. I had no idea how much money I was going to need in Brazil. At one point I felt a twinge of conscience. I wondered if this was drug money or cootchie money that Mayhem had amassed.

"What benefit a man, if he gains the world and loses his soul?" crossed my mind. Then I pushed the thought aside. How much money that circulated in society had its origins in drug money? Was the source of the money I was trying to get released for ransom money for Mayhem drug money? I didn't know anything anymore. All I knew was I had to try to get my brother released. I still had an hour and a half to wait for my plane's departure. I called Chica. "Did you find anything on that tat?"

"Yeah, it sounds like it belongs to your man's family."

"How do you know?"

"It's an old family out of East Los Angeles. I think it's his uncle's and cousins' family— that's why his surname is different. They seem almost like a secret society, they are so below the radar, but they are treacherous, from what I've heard over the years. Do you think Romero knows anything about the abduction?"

"I don't think so, but I can't find out right now. I'm getting ready to take a plane to Rio."

"Where's that?"

"Brazil."

"That far?"

"It's what I have to do."

"Is it for Mayhem?"

"Yes. That's all I can tell you right now."

"This is serious. I'm going to burn a candle for your safe return. Love you, Z."

"Love you too."

I hung up and glanced around. I wanted to call Romero and ask him if he knew if his family had abducted and was holding my brother hostage, but something stopped me. What if it was his family? Would he tell me? Whose side would he take in matters of the heart? Besides, even if he sided with me, could Romero get Mayhem released without the money?

I feel like all my efforts to find out about the kidnapping had led to failure, but, at least, I had tried, even if it was to no avail. Plus, I was really getting frightened. Was someone following me? How did they know I would be at my office? What kind of monster was I dealing with anyway?

I gazed surreptitiously around me. To my left, I observed what looked like a grandmother traveling with two preschoolers. It made me think of Venita and my nephews, and if they were safe. I wondered where she'd taken the boys. I noticed a group of Boy Scouts. I also saw a group of Chinese college students. There was no one suspicious looking around me, but my gut was churning like it does when something's not quite right.

Well, small wonder. I was right out in the open. I was sitting in the boarding area for Delta. I was a sitting duck. I only had my cell phone to take pictures with. I had my small carry-on bag with my big blue Alcoholics Anonymous book, and *The Art of War*. I was going to need all then help I could get.

All of a sudden I got a text from Venita: We safe. I'll contact you when we get settled.

I smiled against my will and had to begrudgingly admit a little feeling for my mother with her stepping up to the plate like this. Here she was, just getting settled in life after twenty years imprisonment, and now she had to be on the lam with her grandsons, who she really didn't know from Adam. All this, once again, for her precious Mayhem, though. Suddenly I felt a sliver of resentment. Almost immediately, I felt guilty for feeling jealous. Mayhem was the one of her children whose life was on the line. Still, I wondered something. Would my mother do the same for me if I were the one being held hostage?

She had tried to reach out to me all my life. She wrote letters to me for twenty years but I'd refused to write her back. Since she'd been out of the pen, she'd tried to be there for me, in her own way.

So what should I do?

I pretended to look out the large windows and listened to the gargantuan jumbo jets take off. But, trust and believe, I had eyes in the back of my head. I used a small compact mirror in my purse to look behind me. I never saw anyone suspicious looking at me. I turned back around and sat down, pretending to read a magazine, although I spent my time studying people out of the corner of my eyes.

As I said, this was my first flight since 9/11. I'd flown more as a child when I'd gone on Caribbean and Hawaiian cruises with Shirley and Chill and the other foster children than I'd flown as an adult. I was pleasantly surprised to be seated in first class this time. I guessed it wouldn't make any difference if the plane went down whether I was first class or coach, but this felt better, since I didn't know what I was going up against or what I'd have to face.

I let out a sigh of contentment, loosening up my jeans' top button. I had plenty of room to stretch out. For a moment, I decided to put my problems aside and luxuriate in all this space.

I prayed as the plane took off, since I'd always heard that was the most dangerous part—take off and landing, but once the plane leveled off, I calmed down. Then I thought about 9/11, and had to calm myself down again. I used self-talk to bring myself back down. I guess I didn't have to worry about terrorists, the way they checked everyone getting on the plane.

When the flight attendant came through taking orders, she asked if I wanted to order a drink, and I was almost tempted to say yes, but I said, "No."

I reviewed the chain of events over the past forty-eight hours. The Academy Awards ceremony. The two federal agents' strange appearance. Mayhem Skyping me. The information I learned from Tank. Moving my nephews to my mother, hopefully to safety. The information from F-Loc. The tattoo shop. The strip club. The massage parlor. Bonzo's henchman. And worst of all, Tank's beheading. It was too much for me to figure out what the pattern was yet, so I tried to quiet my thoughts.

What a moral quagmire! I'd already done something against my honor when I didn't turn in Tank's head. What was the right thing to do?

I opened *The Art of War* and words jumped out at me regarding strategy being more important than fighting in a battle. I was too tired to read, to concentrate, or to think, though, so I rested my head back and closed my eyes. I wondered what this trip would bring. How would I get in touch with Appolonia? I wondered if that shot or that malaria pill was why I was feeling so spacey.

I must have dozed off because suddenly I was nine years old again. I had awakened early one morning to Venita pacing the floor. "That boy has stayed out all night," she mumbled more or less to herself.

I overheard Strange walk up to Venita and say, "That li'l nigga too grown. He may be out here slangin' that rock with these Crips, but I'ma show him. I'ma beat his ass when he get in here. You may be scared of his ass, but I ain't."

Finally, shortly after sunup, Mayhem came slipping through his bedroom window, one ten-year-old leg at a time. Unfortunately, Strange was waiting on the other side of the window for him with an ironing cord. Mayhem took a few licks, but as soon as he broke loose from under Strange's wailing cord, he caught the belt in his hand. In a swift move of the hand, Mayhem pulled out a knife and swiped at Strange.

Strange backed up, grabbing his upper arm. "This li'l nigga done cut me. I'ma kill him when I get my hands on him."

Mayhem made it lickety split to the front door, and stopped at the threshold, but not before he left a threat, which turned out to be a promise. "You ever touch my mother again, I'll kill you. You touch me again or even look at my sister wrong, I'll dead you."

Mayhem shot back out the front door, never to return, other than when Strange was at work so he could check on me, my baby brother, Diggity, and my mother, who was pregnant with my baby sister, Righteousness. From that point, though, he was on his own. I guess it's true. There can't be two men in one house. Mayhem became a man from the time he was ten years old.

That's when the dream went back to the day my daddy died. "Be careful, li'l girl," my father was saying.

Suddenly I felt a gentle hand shaking me. "Are you all right, miss?" I looked into the freckled face of a thin strawberry-blond flight attendant. "You were crying out."

I was sweating profusely and panting. Eyes bucked, I sat up, staring wildly all around me. When I saw I was still on the plane, I calmed myself down, and relaxed, pushing my back into my seat. I was safe—for now.

Chapter Seventeen

When I first landed at the Rio de Janeiro/ Galeão-Antonio Carlos Jobim International Airport, I might as well have landed on Jupiter, I was so in awe. My first impression of Brazil was that it was like what I imagine parts of the Motherland—Africa—would look like. There were people who looked like pure Africans. I guessed they were the ones who I resembled the most.

Then there was another rainbow mixture of all races. The people were bronze, ivory, amber, persimmon, and ochre. What I noticed most were the young women, men and children were exceptionally good-looking. This was a land of beautiful people, I decided. Even the old people looked attractive. Maybe they got the best of the gene pool in the world. I didn't know.

Mainly, I saw people who looked like me as I made my way to the Delta terminal to pick up my suitcase. It was the strangest feeling. On the one hand, I felt like a stranger, but on the other, I felt at home.

I had looked Brazil up online on the flight down. Brazil had the largest Black population other than Africa. This was where the first slave ships stopped. However, the Blacks still had the least political power.

First, I went through customs, which was a half-hour process. The time passed by quickly because I was mesmerized by the sights and the sounds. The smells of fried cassava and banana filled the airport from the street vendors. The unidentifiable smells of different foods from the shops insides the airport made me hungry and my stomach growled. The sounds of the language colored the air like an international Tower of Babel. I saw people of all races.

After I got my suitcases, I panned the crowds looking for someone holding a sign for me. Finally, I saw an attractive woman who looked to be in her late forties holding a sign. "Zippora Saldano." My name was spelled wrong; however, I'd been waiting for an hour, so I was relieved. I'd never been this far away from home, and I was a stranger in a strange new country. Unfortunately, this was no vacation either. I had no gun. All I had were my wits. I felt tensed up inside and tried to relax.

"Here I am," I said, flagging my hands and arms up and down. The lady put her sign down and came forth with a tentative smile. At the same time, I noticed a sadness tugging in the corner of her mouth.

"Hello. Are you Zipporah? I'm Esmeralda, Appolonia's grandmother." She spoke a lilting English with a strong accent, but I understood her, so I was relieved.

Did she say grandmother? She didn't look old enough to be a grandmother. "Yes, I'm Zipporah. Call me Z, though. You look too young to be a grandmother."

"Actually, I'm a great-grandmother. We all had our children young. I'm fifty-four. My daughter is forty and Appolonia is twenty-eight. The sad thing is my daughter is dying." Her face crumpled and I thought of Trayvon. "You never expect to bury your child before you."

"I'm sorry to hear that."

We looped our way in and out through the throngs of people, until we made it the curb. Esmeralda grabbed my small roller bag, hoisted it up, and put it in the back of her Volkswagen bug. She drove past the white sandy Ipanema beach, the sparkling ocean, the palm trees with their fronds flowing in the breeze. Acacia trees lined the streets, and I saw the famous baobab "bottle" trees. I saw exotic-looking birds with bright yellow, green, and blue feathers. I watched the waltzes of large birds of prey, the falcon and the eagles, in the clear emerald sky. The fragrance of nutmeg and cinnamon filled the surrounding markets where people haggled and bargained for prices.

Finally Esmeralda turned into a city I learned was called Rocinha. Rocinha was a favelo (a slum) nestled in the foot of a mountain. In the distance, you could see the famous statue of Christ the Redeemer from the Corcovado mountain in the backdrop of Rio.

The favelas appeared to be part of a maze of shantytowns. Appolonia's *abuela,* Esmeralda, took me to her modest home. I was just amazed how close all the homes were together in the favelas.

As soon as we rounded a narrow street on a hill, I heard the staccato rat-tat-tat of gunshots. The noise reminded me of an AK-47. A large army tank was nestled on one side of the hill, and return fire flashed from the other side of the hill. My ears went deaf and tingled from the blast.

"What the—" I caught myself to keep from cussing. "What's going on?" I asked, ducking for cover. That's all I needed was to come this far and get killed in crossfire.

"Z, keep your head down. The soldiers are fighting the drug traffickers. They're trying to clean up the favelas before the 2014 World Cup and 2016 Olympics."

Out of nowhere, a man, who darted out in front of our car, was hit by a barrage of bullets in the back and dropped dead in front of my face. Thunderstruck, I was speechless for a moment. Esmeralda just speeded up, pulled around the body, and kept driving. She just acted like this was an everyday occurrence. My goodness! They were dropping bodies over here like in South Los Angeles.

"What in the hell was that?" I couldn't hold in my cussing a minute longer. My throat felt as dry as sandpaper. My lungs were wheezing from the shock.

"That was a known drug trafficker. We don't know nothing and we don't see nothing here, if you know what's good for you. Hurry up. Let's get inside." Esmeralda pulled up to a grey adobe-looking building that was connected to other houses.

Once we made it safely inside her modest Spanish home with a glazed red tile roof, I was relieved. It was a shotgun house, with the rooms aligned in a phalanx. The quarters were small, but neat, clean, and orderly. A shrine, which held several candles and a crucifix, was seated in one corner. Two parakeets tweeted in a harmonic blithe song in an ivory cage by the window.

A picture of an attractive teenage girl smiling shyly into the camera stood on a mantle. "Who is she?" I pointed to the picture.

"Orchid. She's my granddaughter. Appolonia's sister."

"I thought you said you were a great-grandmother."

Esmeralda didn't answer. She began cooking something which smelled heavenly. "We're having *feijoada*."

"What is that?"

"Stew."

When we sat down to eat, Esmeralda bowed her head in prayer and held my hand. As soon as I dipped the spoon in my mouth, I found this dish arguably to be the best stew I'd ever eaten. It was made with black turtle beans and various cuts of pork and beef, served with rice and collard greens and a deep-fried cassava and banana.

Throughout the meal, I could hear bullets whizzing and exploding. If I thought L.A. was like a little war time Afghanistan, I was wrong.

Rio had L.A. beat hands-down. I guess I'd come to Rio at the wrong time. At any given moment, gunfire erupted between the security forces or police blitzes and the drug traffickers. I heard gunshots all through the meal until I gratefully was able to tune it out.

After our meal, Esmeralda sat down in the living room and she was ready to talk. She spoke in a hushed tone. "I thank you so much for coming to help us."

What did she just say? I thought. Who said I was going to be able to help them? And who was "them"?

"You're going to have to meet with Diablo and talk to him. Please help get my grand-daughter back."

Chapter Eighteen

I stared at Esmeralda. "First of all, I came here to try to get my brother freed as a hostage. What is going on with Appolonia? Who is Diablo?"

"You don't know of Diablo?"

I remembered the words of the DEA agent, Richard Braggs. "No, but I just heard his name mentioned before I left the States. I heard he is a big fish."

Esmeralda blew air from one nostril in a gush of disgust. She lowered her voice to a whisper. "He's a really big drug lord down here. He got out of prison last year and it's like he didn't miss a beat after being gone almost fifteen years. He ran his organization from the prison, and now he's picked back up from where he left off."

"Why is he holding Appolonia? Does he want money?"

"I don't think so."

What happened to the money she had? I wondered. "First, can you tell me what you know about Appolonia?" I decided to try to get all the information I could.

"She was a sweet girl."

"When was the last time she came home?"

"She hasn't been home in fourteen years."

"Why?"

"I can't talk about it."

"Look, I've got to know what I'm up against. I'm putting my life on the line to help her and my brother. Otherwise, I will get on the plane and go on back to America." I was adamant.

Esmeralda hesitated before speaking. She cleared her throats several times, as if speaking out would put her granddaughter's life in jeopardy. "Okay, as for Orchid, she's not Appolonia's sister. That's her daughter. She had her when she was young. I'm Orchid's great-grandmother. When she was thirteen, Appolonia had gotten involved with Diablo just when he was starting out. At that time, he was growing his cartel. He became a big drug lord and the police wanted him bad. He was living high. Big mansion. Swimming pool. Flaunting it before the poor."

"What happened?"

"When Appolonia became pregnant with Orchid, she was arrested with Diablo. To keep from going to prison while pregnant and giving birth in prison, she turned state's evidence on Diablo. My daughter, Axa, and I kept the baby when she delivered, and Appolonia went to stateside and was put in the witness protection program. Her real name is Samaria."

"So what made her come home now?"

"Her mother is dying and she came home to see her on her death bed. She also wanted to see her daughter, whom she left with me when she was a week old. We acted as if Orchid was Samaria's sister, and my grandchild to keep Diablo from coming after her. I helped my daughter Axa raise Orchid. Anyhow, Diablo went to prison for fifteen years, got out last year, and was determined to get revenge on my granddaughter. When he found out she was with Mayhem, he set up the deal so he could entrap her. He changed his name and now goes by Escobar."

No wonder I couldn't find a long record of Appolonia in the States. She'd been given a new identity. "Didn't she know it was dangerous to come here?"

"She wanted to see her mother and her child," Esmeralda said simply. I guessed because I didn't have a close relationship with my birth mother and didn't have any children, this was kind of unfathomable for me.

"Well, she has money that belongs to the Feds, supposedly, and some Mexican cartel is holding my brother to kill him if they don't get that money—soon."

"So her David has been kidnapped too?"

"Yes. Are you sure they haven't asked for money for Appolonia?"

"No. I believe this is a case of 'if I can't have her, you can't have her either.' Although Diablo was hell bent on revenge, he hasn't harmed her—so far. She's still a beautiful woman. She's already worked her charms on him because he's given her permission to go to the Carnival this weekend."

"How do you know?"

"She sent a message by one of Diablo's men who befriended her. She will be in the Samba Parade. She is still as beautiful as Miss Universe. She is also to be at the ball."

I guessed she was trying to help her man, Mayhem, get back up on his feet too. She apparently stuck by Mayhem when he did some time the year before.

We went to what I assumed was a hospice and visited Axa, Esmeralda's dying daughter. There appeared to be three other patients in the house. We were met by an Amerindian, who wore a long single plait down her back. The house had a hushed tone to it.

The woman didn't appear to speak Portuguese or English. "This is Idina," Esmeralda introduced her. "She is from the rainforest. She was brought here with some nuns when she was a young girl, but she has become like the village healer. She knows all the plants and herbs. The secrets of the jungle."

"What is wrong with Axa?"

Her mother sighed. She put her hands together as if she was praying, looked up to the ceiling, and shook her head hopelessly. "Ovarian cancer."

"Has she seen a doctor?"

"Yes. She has had the chemo and radiation at the big American hospital. It only weakened her more. The doctors sent her home to die. Idina's been caring for her for the past couple of months. No one expected my child to make it this long. I believe she's waiting for Samaria before she lets go."

"Has Appolonia—I mean Samaria been to see her yet?"

"We were trying to get Samaria home so she could say her good-byes, and then she was abducted. She wasn't at the airport when we arrived; we didn't know where she was until she sent the note. We got information from David that he was sending you down to help free her. They say you're a police."

"No, I'm not a policewoman anymore. I'm a PI—a private investigator."

"They say if anybody could help, it's you."

We went inside a small room with only a dresser, a bed, and a pitcher of water. The shades were pulled and the room was dark. Strangely, there was a light that emanated around the patient's face. "Axa, sweetheart, this is Zipporah Saldano. She's from stateside. She is going to help us get our little Samaria back."

Axa's eyes were sunken in. Dark quarter moons shadowed beneath each eye like a raccoon and her lips were chapped, parched looking. Her nose looked pinched. Her face contorted in pain. Her voice was so low, I could hardly hear her. "Does she know?" she mouthed.

Esmeralda leaned in. "She knows. Don't worry. She's on our side. She's David's sister."

"What does she want to know if I know?" Shoot. There were so many secrets I didn't know which one Axa was talking about. First, was she talking about knowing that Appolonia's child was Orchid, or was she talking about the witness protection program?

"Everything. I've told you everything now."

Later, I learned that Mayhem had helped Appolonia send money from an unnamed anonymous source throughout the years so they couldn't trace it back to Samaria.

Now I wondered if Mayhem knew about Appolonia's past.

Chapter Nineteen

The first night I slept in Orchid's room on her narrow bed with the mahogany headboard, Esmeralda gave me a plump round orange. "Put this under your pillow," she instructed.

I looked at her strangely. "Why?"

"Because this is what the Santera told me you must do to cleanse yourself before going into battle."

I was too tired to argue, so I did as I was told, then I conked out and fell asleep. I had no idea what she was talking about.

The next morning, Esmeralda shook me awake. I was met by the beautiful sound of the two parakeets whistling, twittering, and singing. Their songs decorated the air.

"May I have the orange back?" Esmeralda asked.

"What orange?" I asked groggily. I had to reorient myself to my surroundings. Then I remembered I was in Rio, and pulled the orange from under my pillow.

I climbed out of bed, then took a quick bath. Esmeralda told me to hurry and dress and to bring one of my outfits I could afford to lose. I picked out a pair of torn jeans (I'd bought them that way) and a faded T-shirt.

It was still dark as we drove toward the mountain that you could see from all over the city during the daytime. A full moon helped light the way. We finally stopped in front of a whitewashed house that looked like a small cathedral. Amid the rest of the hovels, the place looked like the Taj Mahal. We went inside a darkened room with candles lit all over the room. A strong smell of sage wafted throughout the room.

"Z, this is the Santera. She is so powerful, we don't even call her by name."

The woman, whose skin was ageless and who could have been any age from forty to seventy, was dressed like a gypsy and had a large mole in the middle of her head. This was called the third eye, Esmeralda later explained to me.

I'd heard of the religion Santeria before, but I didn't realize people still practiced it. The Santera spoke in Portuguese, but I understood some of her words because of the similarity to Spanish. Even so, Esmeralda translated for me to be sure I understood what this witch doctor was saying.

"I'm glad to see you. I've got to cleanse your aura. I see a dark cloud surrounding you. You had something bad happen to you when you were a child. Someone you loved died."

I cringed and didn't say anything.

"His name was Butty, but you still have a close relationship. He says to tell you, you're not to blame for his death. That you've always felt guilty, but you're not at fault. It was just his destiny. He wants you to live and to carry on his legacy. He wants you to have children so his line will go on."

Now that's when I became afraid. What kind of voodoo was this? How did she know about my father?

"Do you have the orange you were supposed to sleep with under your pillow last night?"

I pulled out the orange and tried to hand it to the Santera. She didn't touch it.

"Put it on the floor and step on it."

Confused, I didn't know what to think, but I complied. I smashed the orange with my foot; then the Santera picked it up and opened the mashed fruit.

She showed it to me and turned to Esmeralda. I gasped out loud, hand over my heart. "Oh, my God! What is that?"

A face the size of a beetle leered back out at me. It was the visage of an evil-looking man who looked like what I imagined the devil looked like, inside the orange pulp. *How did that get in there?* I wondered. I knew this orange had not been cracked. I shook my head in incredulity.

"That's Diablo!" Esmeralda hissed, her hand over her mouth.

I felt the blood draining from my face. I grimaced in fear of the unknown. I knew there were things that couldn't be explained scientifically, but I'd just witnessed some things I'd never learned in the Western world.

The Santera's voice continued in a hypnotic chant. "Well, this is something I can break. This is a curse Diablo put on Appolonia and

indirectly on you, so this is from man. This is
not a curse from God. I can break a curse from
man."

"I don't understand."

Esmeralda held up her hand, beckoning for
me to be quiet.

The Santera's eyes rolled back into her head
and she started chanting as if she were in a
trance. A weird feeling permeated the room
and my skin prickled. I stood, frozen to the
spot. The eerie howl of a dog in the distance
broke my freeze frame. I shook my head, trying to see if I could get out of this nightmare,
but I looked down, touched my hands, and saw
this was real life. I was not dreaming. I was still
alive.

"I want you to bury these clothes in your
backyard. Put dirt on them to break this curse.
Bring back this box afterward and put as much
money in it as you can. I will then bury the box
in the graveyard."

I didn't care what Esmeralda said, but I felt
the money was for the Santera. I remembered
my thought about how her house was like the
Taj Mahal compared to all the hovels in the
neighborhood around her.

"If anyone comes and talks to you who is a
stranger, don't talk to them. They are straight
from the devil. They may come to you as child
begging but don't pay them any attention. You
are to drink this potion I have mixed for you to
help cleanse you. Someone wanted to kill you
to have put this type of curse on you. They also
have it on Samaria."

"Go to the Carnival and you will find Samaria. Right now she is being held against her will. She will be part of the Samba Parade, and will be on a gold float with a horse like Helen of Troy, and then she will go to the Magic Ball at the Copacabana Palace. Wear this amulet for protection. You must help her escape. It won't be good if she doesn't get away."

The Santera stood up and put this rank, rancid-smelling necklace over my head. It was shaped like the African ankh, like the ring I'd seen Erykah Badu wear. I understood the ankh stood for the symbol of life. For some it was eternal life. Next, I drank something from a goblet that tasted like mud, and hoped it didn't kill me. Right away my stomach began to gripe.

"This will clean you out," the Santera said. "Get home and get to the bathroom."

On our way out, I asked Esmeralda, "Did you tell the Santera that Appolonia had contacted you with a note?"

"No, I didn't."

A chill riveted down my spine.

As soon as we left the Santera's house, what appeared to be a monsoon swooped down on us. One minute it was clear, and the next minute we were in a downpour. I wasn't used to this type of torrential rain and I dashed to the car, mud and water circling around my ankles. I clenched my fist, nerves on edge, as Esmeralda inched down the hills in such pouring rain, but she seemed used to it. The palm trees almost bent to the ground, the wind was so high. I didn't know if we were going to run into a flashflood or what. Now if I was still drinking, this would clearly be a time to need a drink.

"Any questions?" Esmeralda asked.

"Your yard is so small. Where will we get the dirt?"

"Don't worry. We'll get it. I'll return the box for you so the Santera can bury it at the grave-yard so you can go to the Carnival tonight."

"How much money should I put in the box?"

"How much can you afford?"

"I will put $1,000 in the box."

Esmeralda nodded in approval. I knew this sounded crazy, but I felt I had nothing to lose.

Chapter Twenty

"Are you sure you don't want me to stay with you?" Esmeralda said, as she dropped me off at the Carnival later that afternoon.

"No, I work alone. You need to be at the house, just in case Appolonia sends another message."

"Here," Esmeralda said, "Take this. This is the note she wrote to me, letting me know she would be at the Carnival. Also, I've written a note telling her who you are. Here's a map to get a cab to get you back home, if you don't find Samaria. If you find her, take her to her mother's at this address."

Esmeralda hugged me closely. "Make sure you use the amulet the Santera gave you." Esmeralda had explained to me that the Sambadrome Marquês de Sapucaí or simply Sambadrome, also known as the Apoteose Square, was a purpose-built parade area in downtown Rio de Janeiro, Brazil where samba schools parade competitively each year during Carnival.

I'd gone to the Mardi Gras in New Orleans once in my early twenties, but I'd never witnessed such an extravaganza as the Carnival in Rio. It was such a spectacular street party, for a moment I almost, but not quite, forgot my fear.

The trucks with national music blasting from them followed the different floats.

Esmeralda had loaned me a sequined fuchsia-colored and lime costume, which resembled a mango and kiwi fruit. I had tucked my iPhone in the pants of the costume. I decided to leave my passport at Esmeralda's house—just in case. I was to blend in with the dancers of the Blocos Afros who were dressed in bright fruit colors. These were the darker dancers, whom I resembled.

Working my way into the group of dancers who wore the watermelon, melon, kiwi outfits, I held my stomach. I was glad the gripes had past. I finally understood what the Santera meant by "cleansing me out." I'd stayed in the bathroom most of the day, until it was time to get ready for the Carnival.

"Who are you?" one of the samba school instructors asked me as I eased in with her group.

I had to think fast. "I'm the alternate. I'm taking—"

She interrupted me. "Okay. Good. I'm glad they sent someone to replace Letty. Come on let's get in our places."

"Ladies, we've got to win this time. Come on, let's do this!" The instructor turned away, clapping her hands for order.

Fortunately for me, I knew how to samba. Occasionally, Romero and I went out to a Latin club where we would samba.

I found the sight to be breathtaking as the parade of samba schools danced and swiveled up the street. It seemed like one big, moving

organism as the crowds swayed in the bleach-
ers and cheered. A sudden spurt of adrenaline
coursed through my veins. I was getting hyped
by the music and the crowds myself.

I regretted I didn't have my camera. All I had
was my iPhone, which would lose its signal every so often, but I took pictures with it the best
I could, trying not to seem conspicuous. From
what I was told, Appolonia would be wearing a
lime-green feathery costume. She would stand
out because she would hold a white feather that
was different from the others in her group.

I really wished I had my gun, but I just had
to do what I could with what I had to work
with. Truth be known, I had no idea what I
was going to do, but I tried to map out a strategy. *The Art of War* said a good soldier could
win the war without a fight. Surprise could be
your best weapon. I itemized in my head what
I had to do: 1) Find Samaria. 2) Get her to her
dying mother's bedside. 3) Get the money to
release Mayhem. 4) Get out of dodge myself in
one piece. It really wasn't the best of strategy.
I absently fingered the amulet the Santera had
given me. I had no idea how this thing would
play out.

The orange ball of sun had almost dipped into
the ocean before I spotted Appolonia's float. I'd
left the dance group and started following it on
the stands. When the float turned to go to the
hotel, I caught a cab and had the driver take me
to the Copacabana Palace.

Once there, I waited in the shadows at the ball
and watched with interest. I was surprised to see

that it was a black tie and formal dress event. All the attendants were from the upper class, or so it seemed. The dancers were still dressed in full masquerade costumes. When I finally recognized Appolonia and got close enough, I called out her name. She wore a gardenia over her ear, Billie Holiday style. Although darker, she favored the oldest sister, Lonette McKee in the movie *Sparkle*.

"Appolonia. Come with me. I'm Mayhem's sister. He sent me for you. We're going to get to safety."

Appolonia looked skeptical at first. "What? Who are you?"

Thank goodness her mother had given me the note she sent them and she also had handwritten a note that David sent me there to help her. I thrust it at her.

Once Appolonia recognized her mother's handwriting on the note, the light of recognition rose up in her beautiful face.

"Does my David know I'm being held against my will? Good. I was so afraid he thought I'd betrayed him. Never. I love him."

"Well, come on." I pulled Appolonia's arm and we tried to ease into the center of the crowd. We started trying to dance our way in a zigzag, backward line through the crowd, working our way to the entrance. My masquerade costume blended in with the dancers.

At first we were just walking fast, throwing in a samba move once in a while with our hips rolling from side to side. Then we started trotting, and finally, we broke into a jog. Once we were outside the hotel, we broke into an all-out straight run. I felt like someone was following us.

"Halt!" an authoritative voice bellowed. We both stopped running and looked around to see where the voice was coming from. I was scared witless at the loud voice. My heartbeat sped up.

A black police officer marched up to us, and held us at gunpoint. "Halt! Where are you two going? What are you running for? What have you done wrong?"

Before my eyes, I watched Appolonia transform into this femme fatale. She batted the longest sooty eyelashes, dropped her beautiful almond-shaped eyes, and just oozed sensuality. "Officer, I just got word from my friend here that my mother is dying. She's asking for me. I've got to get to her bedside."

The officer paused, but tears welled up in Appolonia's eyes. I knew she wasn't faking those tears. Those were real. "My mother was the best mother a child could have. I've been out the country and I haven't seen *mi mamí* in fourteen years."

"Too bad." The officer seemed nonplussed at first. "I'm still going to have to take you in and run a check on you two. You're showing suspicious behavior. You could be a terrorist."

My heart leaped into my throat.

"Do you have any identification?"

"I have my passport," Appolonia responded. "Officer, don't you have a mother?" She tried to appeal to his sense of decency.

I could see the officer wavering—unsure of what to do. He seemed hypnotized as he eyed

Appolonia with lust. Her costume, like many of the dancers at the Carnival, was very provocative. Her narrow waistline was draped in gold-trimmed pearls, and her low-cut sheer top revealed an ample bosom. He stared her curvy body up and down and licked his lips like she was a pork chop.

All of a sudden, to the far west, the staccato of gunshots rang out in the air. It sounded like firecrackers on the Fourth of July.

Random shouts pierced the air. "He's got a gun!"

"Run!"

"It's a sniper."

The officer turned in the direction of the shots. He got a call on his walkie-talkie. "Sniper. Trouble near the Palace."

"Okay, I'll check it out." Totally distracted, the officer turned on his heel and sped off, never looking back at us.

"Come on, let's run," I whispered to Appolonia, grabbing her by the arm. We ran in the opposite direction. "Come with me!"

"Where are we going?"

I spoke tersely. "I'm trying to get you to your mother's. She's holding on to see you. Also, they are holding Mayhem until you send the ransom money that you were supposed to do the deal with Diablo."

Appolonia nodded. "I still have the money in an account."

Before I could get happy over this, I saw a man in the corner of my eye, moving aggressively toward us.

"Run!" I shouted. "I think someone's spotted us."

For some reason, I had a feeling that that shooting in the air was just a diversion for the police and a way to get us out of his clutches so our pursuers could get at us. *Might as well have leaped out the frying pan into the fire*, I thought. We didn't get arrested but now we were about to get caught by assailants, whom I assumed were Diablo's men.

We ran as fast as we could, huffing and puffing, jostling people. I was glad I was in shape from the tae kwon do, but running in heels was not the most conducive to being swift.

"Take off your heels," I called out, as I stopped and took my heels off and threw them aside. I picked back up my pace. Appolonia did the same, and kept trotting behind me. We broke our way through the crowd of partying people.

We hadn't run two city blocks when two cars screeched in front and in back of us. Three men, armed with nine millimeters with silencers, leaped out the car and bum-rushed us.

"Get in the car, bitch. Both of you." The lead goon pushed me by the shoulder into the back seat of a black sedan.

Chapter Twenty-one

The last thing I recalled was someone putting a handkerchief, which smelled like chloroform, over my nose, when I hit the back seat of the car. After that, I was out like a light.

Off in the distance, I saw a tunnel of light and my father was standing in front of it. Then suddenly, he materialized before me. He looked like he did before the last time I saw him with his chest blown out.

"Baby girl, be careful," he said. "You've got to wake up. You're going to have to be strong and help yourself."

I could feel him fading away. I reached out my hand to him. "Daddy, I want to go with you."

"It's not time. You have to go back."

"Why can't I go with you?" *I asked.*

"You have work to do. I want you to promise me something."

"What?"

"Never be a victim."

"Okay, Daddy, but don't leave me."

"I'll never leave you. I'm always inside of you."

I didn't know how much longer it was before I woke up, but when I did, I was somewhere in a darkened room. I tried to remember what had happened. I was sure someone had drugged me.

Where was I? I tried to move, and couldn't budge. That's when I realized I was tied up. I was laying sprawled out, spread eagle into a Y shape on what felt like a king-sized bed. I was lying on a thick quilt. My hands were manacled on each side and both legs were bound. I wiggled and struggled to do all I could, but the ropes wouldn't give and I couldn't get loose. My head was hurting so bad I couldn't worry about the danger I was in. I felt sore inside, as if I'd been raped, but I wasn't sure.

Talking about a freak accident! Now here I came to Brazil to try to help free my hostage brother's hostage wifey, but instead, I'd wound up kidnapped too. Possibly raped. *Ain't this a bitch?* Forgive me, Lord, but I had to cuss. I guess I got caught up in a hostile takeover, because obviously, these people wanted Appolonia. I was a hostage by association. Now I really could choke Mayhem for the mess he'd gotten me into. I was in the belly of the beast. I thought of Romero and wished I'd told him I would marry him when he asked.

I was in a country I knew nothing about, and in a world, that from all appearances, was hell.

Then I remembered what I came to Rio for in the first place. The ransom money. Mayhem's kidnappers said I only had a week to get this money and get back to L.A. How was I going to be able to do that now?

Determined to get free, I shifted around on the bed. I could feel the amulet that was around my neck move. I moved and squirmed my body around again, trying to locate my phone, which had been latched to a belt inside my costume. I couldn't find my phone. I wanted my iPhone so I could somehow get in touch with Romero. I looked down and searched the costume I was wearing and I couldn't find my phone. I remember tucking it down into my costume pants, inside of my passport cover. Now I was grateful I'd left my passport at Esmeralda's.

What was I going to do?

"I hear her moving around in there," I heard a male voice with a heavy accent say.

"Who are you?" a gruff voice demanded. I jumped with a start. The voice sounded all the scarier because the room was dark.

Suddenly a light flashed on. "She's coming to," I heard a voice say in Spanish.

"Yeah, we got to see where's she's from." Another voice piped in. "Samaria said she's an American. Do you think she's a Fed?"

"I don't know."

I squinted as I tried to adjust my eyes to the light. "Who are you?" I asked in return. My voice sounded slurred. My mouth felt like sandpaper. I tried to rake the room, but everything was still kind of blurry.

"Look, I'm asking the questions in here. My boss, Escobar, wants to see you." His English was short, clipped, but I understood him.

Now that I could see, my eyes raked the room. I found out I was tied to a large four poster bed.

Actually, the room was extremely large and decorated with gilded furniture. From what I could surmise, this was a room that was part of a mansion.

The one man took a knife. I held my breath as he cut loose my restraints. I was so afraid he would cut or stab me with the knife. He came close to my wrists, but he didn't cut me.

"Look, who are you? Why are you trying to kidnap Samaria?" he whispered.

I didn't answer. This must be the lie that Appolonia told her captors. I didn't know if he was friend or foe. Now I didn't know what to think about Appolonia. Was she really staying here against her will?

At gunpoint, the two men pushed me toward a flight of winding stairs. My bare feet padded on the dark oak hardwood floor, which felt cold and clammy. My legs were so weak, I stumbled and staggered. I still felt woozy and druggy. I held on to the birch stair rail to keep my balance. I did feel sore inside like someone had touched me, but I wasn't sure. Right now I had to make sure I kept my life.

The men walked with a military gait, and they escorted me under a teak wood high-beamed ceiling, which was one of the main things I noticed. The stairs were dimly lit, so I had to be careful not to fall.

They marched me through a long corridor to the end of the house. We entered a room, which had French doors that opened up to an ocean view. I could see a white stone fence surrounding the property. The terrace outside was surrounded by cactuses, palm trees, and acacia trees. I could see several other houses on the compound. The house looked like part of a villa. It was early morning, judging by the position of the sun.

A swarthy, gruff-faced man with a pock-marked complexion sat at the head of a large Queen Anne desk. He leaned back into his leather wing-back chair, lacing his fingers like the venomous spider with the unsuspecting fly. He was the spider. I was the fly, but I was far from unsuspecting. As I stared in his face, I saw the same visage I'd seen of the beetle inside the orange at the Santera's. I'd been given a sign and a warning. He wore a beard and he reminded me of Castro. I felt like I was in the presence of Satan himself. He was smooth and charming, and had a macho stance. I felt like I was staring in the face of pure evil. "Well, well, well. Zipporah Saldano."

I didn't like how he said my name. I knew I was on the hot seat. I felt like I was a fly caught in his spider's poisonous web. "How do you know my name?"

He paused as if for dramatic effect, then sniffed his glass like a connoisseur. He swished wine on his tongue and assumed a judicial ex-pression as he slowly sipped from an amber wine goblet. He finally spoke. "Samaria told me your name."

"What is your name?"

"Escobar. You're a bold woman." He paused. "I like that in a woman."

I didn't answer. I tried to hide any signs of fear. This was something I'd learn to do well over the years. What was he planning to do with me? Would they torture me or would it be a quick death?

"So you're David aka Big Homie's sister?"

"I thought you wanted to do business with Mayhem—I mean Big Homie."

"I was, but he has something that belongs to me. I have it back now. Tell him I don't want to do business with a thief."

"What does he have that belongs to you?"

"He had Samaria—well, you all knew her as Appolonia. Even with the facial reconstruction she's had, I'd know her anywhere. But now I have her back."

"Why do you feel he took your woman? You were before his time."

"No, you tell your brother this woman is mine." He took a flat hand and pounded his chest. "I raised this girl from a wee girl." He held his hand low like about age ten. "I'm no short eyes, though. I waited until she became a woman at thirteen before I made her mine. I popped her cherry. And you know what they say. You never forget your first. She loves me. She came back to me. I'm willing to forgive her and take her back. She was under duress when she turned state's evidence with me. She will always be mine."

I didn't answer. Did he mean to send me back to the States? I felt a glimmer of hope.

"My lieutenant has an eye for you. He says you're the finest piece of chocolate woman he's ever seen or tasted."

My throat constricted and turned dry as a cotton ball. "And what is that supposed to mean?"

"That means you'll get a little reprieve. You know I could have my men kill you, but if you make my lieutenant happy . . . we'll see. Relax. Trust me." Both of his arms were crossed, indicating he was lying. I just held my face straight.

Trust you? Hah!

I sat and stared at the smug look on his face. He was playing with me like a lion playing with a mouse—until he got ready for the kill.

Chapter Twenty-two

I had to think fast. First, I knew I needed some food. I couldn't fight back on an empty stomach. I couldn't even think clearly. My stomach was growling and I was feeling weaker by the moment. I hadn't eaten since yesterday morning. The potion the Santera made had acted as a laxative so I was emptied out.

"I'd like something to eat, sir, if it's all right with you." I tried to humble my voice the way I saw Appolonia work the police officer. In fact, how she was able to keep this sociopath from killing her after she sent him to prison showed the girl had skills.

"Yes, you must eat. We got plans for you."

I nodded affably, pretending to go along with his program. *The best thing is to twist the facts to your advantage.* "Gracias," I said, using some of my Spanish.

"Okay," Escobar said. "So you speak Spanish."

"A little."

He snapped his fingers and a rotund woman with two long rope braids crisscrossing her head and a portly waddle appeared. "Matilda, bring the lady some breakfast."

Escobar watched in silence as I gulped down a breakfast of pineapples, avocado, mangoes, kiwis, and plantains. I drank almost a gallon of water with a squeeze of lemon from a jade pitcher. My stomach started feeling more settled. I felt my strength return.

"Thank you for your kindness. I'd like to take a bath before I meet the lieutenant. What is his name?"

"Alfredo. You're welcome for the breakfast. *Mi casa es su casa.* Matilda, take her to the bathroom." He snapped his fingers and two of his henchmen appeared. They both were armed with nine millimeters.

"Go to the bathroom with her while she cleans up. Get her some of Appolonia's clothes and get her some shoes."

The men nodded, then accompanied me, at gunpoint, to the bathroom.

As I sat in the large sunken tub filled with hot water, I soaped away the filth oozing from my body and I thought of Romero and I cried. I'd never cheated on him since I'd been with him, as his woman, and, although I was drugged, I hated the thought of another man's hands, let alone body parts, fondling or being in or on my body. This was Romero's "diamond" as he called my sex parts.

I thought back to how I didn't value my body when I was young. Although I was a virgin until I was nineteen (thanks to Shirley's close supervision), when I was almost gang raped at

eighteen, I didn't really understand the reper-
cussions of sexual assault.

At the time, I was willing to give up my vir-
ginity rather than give my three assailants my
money. True, I was concerned with keeping my
money so I could buy gifts for my baby brother
and sister who were in foster care at the time.
Although I scared the guys off, telling them I
was HIV positive, I think what really scared
them off was when Romero came along and
rescued me. I thought about Romero and a
pang went through my soul. Would I ever see
him again? This man was the best man I'd ever
had.

I didn't know where my iPhone was so I
couldn't try to contact anyone. I only had the
amulet the Santera gave me, but what good was
it doing me?

I looked around the room for something I
could use as a weapon. I found a long hairpin
and unbent it. I stuck it in my hair, which I was
glad I'd let grow out so it was hidden. I wondered where Appolonia was in this big house.
The way Escobar acted so smug and self-sat-
isfied, she obviously was not in harm's way at
this moment.

I put on the long red dress with a split on the
side and the golden sandals, which I assumed
were Appolonia's. Although she was shorter
than me, since I'd trimmed down the dress to
fit me. However, the dress came just below my
calves, when it should have been floor-length.

Afterward, the two sentry guards marched
me to my room and roughly pushed me in-

side. I heard the door lock behind me. I double checked and it was definitely locked. Bars enclosed the full-length room windows, so I was trapped.

I sat and scanned the room. I was glad that they did not tie me up again. I studied the four poster bed to see how they had tied me up. Next, I checked the sheets. I didn't see any evidence of sexual activity, so I wondered why I'd felt sore down there. I thought about it. My clothes were still on when I woke up. What was going on? The bedroom floor was made from a terra cotta ceramic tile and I didn't find any loose tiles where I could maybe find a way out.

Then I thought of my more immediate priority. How was I ever going to get out this mess? I still had the amulet—the ankh. I rubbed it and hoped this voodoo mess worked. No way was I going to be given to some man I didn't know, and be conscious, in my right mind. What kind of patriarchal society was this? As far as women had come, it still boiled down to we could easily become victims because of our sexuality. We could still be raped, murdered, or exploited.

Suddenly I remembered my teacher, Miss Golden's, program, "I'm Not Your Victim." Then and there I decided I was not going to be a victim if I could help it. That's how I came up with a plan.

Chapter Twenty-three

A few hours later, a soft knock came at the heavy oak door.

"Who is it?" I asked seductively.

"It's Alfredo." The door slowly cracked opened. An elderly Hispanic male sauntered in. He was neatly dressed in a smoke jacket, a tie, and navy linen serge slacks. He wore his curly hair pulled back and it ended at the nape of his neck. His hair had thinned in the crown and he had liver spots on his hands. He was sepia colored and could pass for just about any race under the sun.

"I'm Alfredo. Thank you for receiving me." His English was halting, but clear. He could have been any normal business man, but this man held my life in his hands.

I smiled, trying to hide my revulsion. I thought of the geisha girls in Arthur Golden's book, *Memoirs of a Geisha,* and I remembered the girls at The Kitty Kat Koliseum. The power of the "P." Women held the power. We just had to play our cards right.

I smiled, pretending to be shy. "You seem tense. Would you like to sit down and talk?"

There was a table and chair in the room in the corner.

"Sure. Would you like a drink?" he asked. He was soft-spoken.

"No. I don't do alcohol anymore. I'd like a cup of tea though."

He went back to the door and had Matilda order tea. Matilda returned with hot tea in two china cups on a tray.

"Well, I'm a business man, and I'll get right to the point. You're the type of woman I'd love to have at my side. I saw you dancing at the Carnival and I loved the way you moved. You seem like a woman with a lot of nerve, too. I mean the way you tried to kidnap my boss's woman . . ."

"What kind of business would you like me to do?"

"You could fly in and out the United States and help transport our product. You won't want for nothing. I have a mansion as big as Escobar's. I will make you a rich woman. Oprah won't have nothing on you."

He pulled out a key and opened a window. The window opened to a balcony with granite balustrades. He took his hand and showed me the mountains, the ocean, and the large neighboring mansions.

I didn't answer. I got up and started dancing a slow samba around the room. I did a slow voluptuous sway, then I'd take a few mincing steps.

I watched Alfredo's eyes widen. He unloosened his tie, and he began to lick his lips salaciously.

"Did you touch me last night?" I asked, giving him a playful wink, as if I had enjoyed it. I threw my hip suggestively toward him. I pivoted and swiveled my pelvis in the samba move.

"No, but I tasted you. I can't wait to get inside of you now. Your lips look like plums down there and you're as sweet as a mango."

Okay, no wonder I felt funny down there. No wonder my clothes were still on. I got sickened at the idea of his old behind touching me that intimately, but I hid my aversion. I continued dancing slowly, sensuously, until he had eased off his slacks and his shirt. I could see his small erection standing out through his shorts. I also noted his gun in the pants. Alfredo took long strides and climbed on the bed. I kept dancing.

"Give it to me, baby," he crooned. He patted the pillow and the sheet. He started talking dirty in Spanish. I made out his words. "Come to me, *mamacita*. Come to *papi*."

"Close your eyes," I cooed seductively.

As soon as Alfredo closed his eyes, I grabbed his nine millimeter gun and got the drop on him. I held it on him while his eyes were still closed.

I took the bobby pin and stuck it in his acupuncture point in his neck. Next, I tossed the hot tea on him, splashing his face and his chest. I pulled the gun and cocked it.

He jumped up off the bed, screaming like a laughing hyena. He grabbed the sheet and was trying to cool off.

"Shut up hollering like a woman or I'll throw another cup on you. This is what you get for taking my sex when I was drugged."

"I'm sorry, but you looked so sexy. I couldn't help myself."

"Oh, the devil made you do it. You keep talking about that shit, I'll kill you on GP. Now where is Appolonia—I mean, Samaria?"

He hesitated.

"Oh, do I have to put a cap in your ass for you to talk?"

His eyes became saucers. He sputtered out, "She's in the room at the end of the hall."

"Do you have a key?"

"No." I cocked the gun again, this time pointing at his little johnson.

He threw both hands up in surrender. He sure didn't want to lose his manhood. "Okay. Okay. Yes, I have it. It's in my pants pocket."

I fished into his pants pocket and found the key. "Is this it?"

He nodded, still glaring at me. Next, I tied Alfredo up with the same rope they'd used on me and gagged his mouth with his own tie. I could see the burn beginning to peel on the left side of his face. It was just a first- or second-degree burn, I decided. His nostrils flared in rage. Although his mouth was muffled, I could make out his words. "I'ma kill you, bitch, when I get free."

"You can lay the pipe on your own self," I quipped over my shoulder. I peeked out the room and didn't see the guards. I kept the gun cocked, and tiptoed down the long hallway. I made it to the door at the end. I took the key and turned it. I found Appolonia alone inside. She was not tied up, and she seemed to be searching the room.

"Zipporah?" She seemed surprised to see me. "How did you get away? I'm so sorry about everything."

"Do you have the money for Mayhem's release?" I went straight to the point. This was the reason I'd come to Rio in the first place. If she was really telling the truth, she'd help me get away.

"Yes, it's in this account." Appolonia got down on the floor and lifted a floorboard. She reached in and handed me a flash drive. "The password is on there too. You can transfer the money to whatever account the kidnappers want."

"What happened to the drugs?"

"There were never any drugs. Escobar just wanted to get me back."

I looked at her incredulously. "Come again?"

"He staged this buy and acted like he was going to be a connect for David. He'd changed his name and I thought it would be safe to come back to say good-bye to my mother and hello to my daughter."

I shook my head. This was deep. "Do you want to stay here?"

"I want to see my mother before she closes her eyes in death. I'd like to see the baby I left behind when I left this place. From there . . . I don't know."

"You know this is putting your life at risk, don't you?"

"When you helped Mayhem, didn't you realize you were putting your life on the line?"

I thought about it. That was so true. But what could you do when it was your loved ones? I didn't answer her question.

"Come on. Pick up your speed. We don't have much time. Do you know where the guards are?"

"After the Carnival, they're having a big meeting. Some big deal they want to do. They only have a skeleton crew back at the hacienda."

"Do you know how to get out of here without us being seen?"

"Yes. He has shown me all over this house, to let me see how big he is—even living larger than he was when I was a teenager. There's an underground passage in the cellar, which lets you out three miles away from here."

Chapter Twenty-four

As we stealthily eased down the steps, for each creak in the floorboards, in every shadow, I saw Escobar or one of his goons, but it was only my imagination. Everyone, except for a few sentry guards left in the front yard, had gone back out to the Carnival. Appolonia said she overheard they were going to have a meeting afterward. I guess Alfredo had been left alone to have his way with me.

We finally managed to get down the back kitchen stairs to the cellar with no problem. Once we eased down the basement stairs, Appolonia showed the way to a dusty carved wood door in the back of a wine cellar, and it opened to an old-fashioned underground tunnel.

We ran for almost a half hour through this darkened damp tunnel until we emerged into a light green and yellow rolling savannah. Acacia trees and shrubs dotted this grassland. Monarch butterflies floated on the wind. A few straggling stray cows grazed in the distance.

"How close are we to the nearest town?" I asked. I shaded my eyes and tried to block the sun glare. Judging from the position of the sun, it was about noon.

"It's about five miles away. We can catch a cab to the hospice from there."

"I've got to get back to your grandmother's to get my ticket and get back to the States." I was relieved to know I had the money to free Mayhem, but now the next problem was how to get out of Rio alive.

"Once we get to town, I'll call my grandmother and tell her to bring your belongings over to the hospice."

"Okay."

"Are you okay, Z?" Appolonia asked.

I paused. The old, pre-AA treatment me would have said, "I'm fine." But I didn't lie. "No, I'm messed up, but we've got to keep it moving before these fools get back. Alfredo's last words were he was going to kill me."

I decided to flip the script and interrogate Appolonia as we pushed our way through the tall grass.

"I asked you, did you want to stay here?"

"No. But I want to see my mother and my daughter. For this reason, I can't go back with you. I've got to stay—for now."

"Escobar may kill you. Are you sleeping with him again?"

"Yes. I'm sorry but I had to make him think I still love him."

"The Santera says he's put a curse on you."

"I don't believe in that old mess. That's my grandmother's thing."

"Well, what do you believe in?"

"What do I believe?" she repeated rhetorically. "I believe in money."

"Is money your God?"

"It's the God of America. Shit. Money's the God of the world. Look at how everyone goes crazy when the stock market crashes globally. People give you respect when you have money. I don't care. I come from nothing and I know I like it when I have money. I promised myself when I was a young girl I would not stay poor, no matter what it took."

"So you're willing to sell your soul to the highest bidder?"

Appolonian didn't answer. She finally spoke up. "If anything happens to me, please help raise my boys."

"If he doesn't kill you, do you plan to come back and get them?"

"I don't know. Where are they?"

"I had my mother get them out of L.A. She's taking them someplace safe."

"Thank you so much. I love my boys."

"Anyhow, I understand only one is your biological son. Why do you have the other two boys? Didn't their mothers want them?"

"No. They just had their babies, trying to trap David. I told him about these gold-digging bitches. He paid his child support and everything, but that wasn't what they wanted. When they couldn't get him to leave me, they just dumped the babies on our doorstep, one by one. I've had them since they were babies."

"Didn't it bother you that Mayhem cheated on you?"

Appolonia shrugged. "It goes with the territory. Powerful men are women magnets. I was the one driving a Bentley."

Hmmm. She sure seemed accepting of Mayhem's whorish ways. "Why have you always been involved with drug dealers?"

"As you see, I grew up very poor. The drug traffickers were the ones with the money."

"How did you get with Diablo in the first place?"

She brushed her curly hair back from her face, as she tried to keep pace with me. "I met him when I was ten or eleven. He was just coming up then. He had his eye on me, even back then. He started out buying me clothes he had shipped from America. He had connections with the men on the ship. He never touched me until my period started."

"But why him? He seems so—so evil."

"When you grow up in the favela, sometimes you don't even have money to buy Kotex. I was a girl who always wanted nice things. I wanted more than my mother and grandmother could give me. I liked going to school dressed in pretty American-made clothes. All the girls would admire my clothes, and ask, 'Oh, how can you afford them?'"

"What did your mother say? Did she ask where you got the clothes from?"

"She worked hard at the clothing factory, sewing all day, and she didn't have any energy to see what I was doing. When she asked, 'Where did you get the clothes?' I would tell her my grandmother gave me the money for sweeping for her. I was what they called a 'useful' child. They used to say, 'Make yourself useful.'

"See, I was one who always swept up and did work for my grandmother at her sewing job, so I told them my *abuela* bought them. But Diablo bought them."

"Well, when you came to America and changed your identity, how come you got with my brother?"

"David has ambition. I always like that about him. He's a business man, just like any man on Wall Street."

"Mayhem is a drug dealer!"

"You think that they don't deal drugs on Wall Street?"

I turned and looked at her. I couldn't answer that question. "Well, why didn't you go to school, get an education, take care of yourself since you were given a second chance? You were in America. The land of opportunity. Right? Why did you hook up with another drug dealer?"

"Look, I know you're judging me. I didn't have a mother or anyone in Los Angeles to guide me. Even when I had a mother and grandmother, I was attracted to Diablo. So this is just me."

"Well, how did you meet Mayhem?"

"I met David shortly after I got to stateside. I was only fifteen. He was just coming up with his business. I started out as a mule for him, and then, when I turned eighteen, I wound up becoming his woman. David is ambitious, he's smart, and he's been good to me. All the women see what me and him have built together and they want to take it. They think he'll do for them what he does for me, but he won't. He's shrewd like that."

"Well, why do you think Escobar didn't re-
taliate against you for sending him away? Most
people in the witness protection program are
targeted if they turn in someone."

"I don't know. He just wants to keep me near.
Now, he may not trust me, but so far, he hasn't
killed me."

"I'll take you to your mother; then I've got to
get out of dodge. If I were you, I would get out
of Rio too."

"I'm not leaving yet. You shouldn't go to the
airport from here. I'll have Idina take you up
the Amazon. You can leave from the airport in
Manaus."

"Who is Idina?" I asked.

"Idina; she's the lady who is taking care of
your mother."

"Yes. She's from one of those unnamed tribes
in the rainforest. She knows the terrain."

Chapter Twenty-five

I watched Appolonia go in to say her good-byes with her dying mother, Axa. Meanwhile, I waited in the living room for Esmeralda to arrive with my traveling bag and my passport.

Esmeralda arrived within fifteen minutes. She handed me my bag and passport. I frisked in my bag, looking for my iPhone; then I remembered I'd taken it to the Carnivale with me. It was missing when I woke up, tied to Escobar's bed. I couldn't worry about that now.

Tears rolled down Esmeralda's face. "Thank you from the bottom of my heart for getting my granddaughter here." Appolonia came in, and the two women broke down crying and hugging at the same time.

Annoyed, I didn't answer. *Yes, I got your granddaughter here to say good-bye to her dying mother, but at what price?* I thought. Now I could never look at my man with the same purity I had before. I would never be able to tell Romero what really happened to me in Brazil, I decided.

As I was leaving the hospice with Idina, I heard the rat-tat-tat-tattat of gunshots. My heart started pounding and my senses all jumped to attention.

Out of the corner of my eye, I saw a group of Escobar's men leap out of a Jeep, two doors down from the house. They were all brandishing their guns.

"There she is! Kill her!" I heard Alfredo's voice rise in a stentorian bellow. The other three men began shooting at me. Obviously, I'd been IDed. Alfredo seemed to hold back and just give the orders.

I pushed Idina back in the house. "Run. Hide!"

In a leap off the porch, I darted and ducked behind a neighbor's car, then cocked my gun. My heart started catapulting in my chest. I took a deep breath, trying to center myself. I pulled on all my experience as a former police and all that I'd learned as a P.I. As a final resort, I remembered my Higher Power. I said a quick prayer, "Lord, help me!"

It was as if a voice spoke out loud to me:

If you want to survive in battle, you have to improvise. The best laid plans will kill you. Remember; the greatest weapon in any battle is surprise.

Gratefully, a spirit of calm settled over me. I stayed in position between the car and a house behind me. I methodically took my time whenever I would shoot. It seemed to have provided a good barricade. I didn't know how many bullets I had, but I didn't want to waste any of them. The first man who came forward toward me was blasting with all his might, and all I saw was a hail of bullets. The booming sounds of the gunshots let me know he had a high-powered nine millimeter. My ears tingled from the loud boom boom sounds of gunfire. I remained calm, though, crouched on my knees in the eye of the storm. Surprisingly lucid, I aimed and fired. I hit my first attacker between the eyes. He didn't exactly know where I was hiding, but now the others knew where I was. I moved farther down to another car.

The second man, seeing his friend fall, seemed unnerved and even more enraged and determined to kill me. He came charging toward me with an indestructible attitude. As a drug lord, I guess he believed in his own myth. That he was larger than life. He just kept coming at me, acting as if he was bulletproof. In his frontal attack, he was shooting aimlessly, though, still walking toward my hiding place. From where I stooped, I saw my advantage. I could see he was losing control he was so livid. I thought he was driven by the nerve of it all. He acted as if how dare I, as a woman, kill his crony?

I was amazed as he stalked straight toward me, as if to say since he was a crime lord, I was supposed to be intimidated. Well, my back was up against the wall, and I had to do what I had to do. I was in the most dangerous space in the world for a person to be. It was called do or die. Me or him. And truthfully, if anyone had a choice between choosing their life over an assailant's life, it would be their life every time.

When he got four feet away, I watched my assailant walk straight into my next bullet, which went straight into his heart. I could see the look of surprise on his face as he dropped to his knees, then crumpled over.

The third man seemed a little intimidated by my marksmanship. He ducked behind a car and shot from there. I studied him as he developed a rhythm. He would dip, then shoot, dip then shoot. I stepped inside his rhythm and waited for him to come up and shoot, and I aimed. Bam. I hit him on the second shot. He collapsed.

After exchanging fire, I realized I'd shot three of the four men who had come after me. I felt detached the whole time. I was in that place in the jungle called "survival of the fittest." I didn't get triumphant feeling, because I knew it was not over.

My artillery was gone. Alfredo was still out there. I paused. How would he come at me? I had to get a grip on my emotions and be ready.

Finally I heard Alfredo calling out, "I'll kill you, bitch. I'm gonna cut you down 'til you'll be too short to shit."

"Not if I kill you first." I gritted my teeth. Blood surged to my fists. I pulled my trigger and it clicked. I was out of ammunition. I sucked my teeth in disgust, then threw my gun down and charged forward, filled with hatred. I was in the belly of the beast and I had to slay the dragon. We hit each other with such force, I heard him let out an "Oomph." We got into hand-to-hand combat.

Alfredo's face was lobster red where I had thrown the hot tea on him, but the purple rage that colored his skin came from a different source—he wanted revenge. His eyes blazed murderously; his veins stood out in livid ridges.

He threw his gun down on the ground. For him to be an older dude, Alfredo was in good shape. He was amped because I had embarrassed him in front of his boys, and I was pumped because of my anger at him for taking advantage of me when I was drugged.

I fought with everything in me. Everything I learned in my tae kwon do class helped me in the fight. We circled each other, and for every thrust Alfredo made at me, I was able to kick and deflect his movement. He knew some form of martial arts too, but I was younger and faster. I was shocked at the calmness that stayed in the center of my mind, but I knew it would be a fight to the finish. Either I would die, or he would die.

Finally I was able to strike Alfredo's carotid artery with the side of my hand turned like a hatchet and watched blood spurt out his mouth. He slumped over on top of me. I pushed him off, trying to keep the blood off me, but I was covered in his blood.

I couldn't believe it! I'd killed a man with my bare hands. My adrenalin, which coursed through my arteries, was just beginning to slow down. I didn't really think about it. I scooped up Alfredo's gun, which still had bullets in it, from the street. I decided to keep it for safety until I reached the airport. I didn't know if they would kill Appolonia or what. She made her choice. I made mine. All the money in the world that Alfredo offered could not buy my soul. Everybody has to make their own choices. All I knew was now I had to get home.

Breathing in ragged snorts, I staggered back into the hospice. I was sore, covered in Alfredo's blood, but I didn't have any marks on me. The mark I had was a deeper scar on my soul.

"Are you okay?" Appolonia rushed to me.

Esmeralda looked shocked. "I've never seen a woman fight like you. You just took down four men. You did what the police here haven't been able to do. Keep that amulet with you."

Dazed, I didn't answer. "Give me my suitcase and my passport. I'm out of here."

My arms hung loosely at my side as the two women hugged me. I felt floppy as a dead fish, eyes wide open, shocked. I was so numb I couldn't even feel my own hands. I glanced down and saw the trigger burns on the inside of my palms.

"Here, put this jacket on," Appolonia said. "You're covered in blood." Samaria slipped a khaki jacket over my shoulders. "Please leave before Escobar gets here. Idina will get you to safety."

Without saying good-bye, I followed Idina as she rushed into her small Tracker Jeep. I climbed in the car and rode in silence as she drove us to the Amazon River.

There was a boat leaving for Manaus when we arrived at the dock. The ride up the Amazon was terrifying and mind-boggling. I was in a single motor boat. The hunter green tree branches hung over the river and you could see strange birds I'd never seen before shoot out. I didn't know what to do. A fog arose from the water and the only light I could see was the one

from the boat and the only sound I could hear
was the one from the motor, putt, putt, putting.

Idina warned, "Keep your hands in the boat.
Look out for snakes. They hang from the trees.
We're going through the rainforest."

I didn't answer. I just shivered and sat covered in a net, the insects were so treacherous.
A mosquito had bitten my neck, and when I
squashed it, I was surprised at the size of the
insect. I felt a stream of blood on my neck, and
I rubbed it absently with my finger.

I was frozen in time. Suddenly we were en-
gulfed in blackness. I was in the heart of darkness. I saw a few tribes on the shore, waving at
us.

"Headhunters. Cannibals," the boat captain
said. I was too numb to be afraid.

It turned so dark, you couldn't see stars; you
couldn't see anything but black. We floated
through different levels of black. Purplish
black. Blue black. Indigo black. We were swallowed up by the wilderness.

My eyes darted about maniacally, trying to
pick objects out of the gloom. Finally the clouds
parted like the Red Sea and a glimmer of moon
eased through the tree branches and the world
turned grey. It was like watching a drop of dew
on a rose petal. You could make out the outline
of the thicket on each side of the river, and I felt
a little more relieved.

All I wanted was to see America again. I
couldn't wait to get back home to the land of
the free, the home of the brave. I didn't know if
I'd ever be the same again.

I was concerned for my brother's release but now, all I wanted to do was to get home safely.

Everything seemed surreal. I think I dozed off, but I remember waking up because, at one point we had to outrun an anaconda, which floated near our boat. I woke up in time to see what looked like a sea monster. I took out my gun and shot three bullets into the huge snake's body.

Afterward, I didn't—no, couldn't—go back to sleep. I felt like I was in hell, and didn't know if I would ever get out safely. Why did I get involved? Why didn't I just agree to marry Romero and lead a safe life? Well, if I made it back safely to America, that's just what I was going to do.

I touched my amulet. What danger lurked in the rainforest? What if Escobar's men followed me up the Amazon? I didn't have my iPhone and the gun only had a couple of bullets left in the chamber.

To tell the truth, I wasn't a religious person, but that day I prayed and meditated like crazy. *In the wilderness, the laws of battle change. I will just sit still and pray. I need courage.* At the end of the day, I just wanted to make it home with as much of my integrity intact as possible.

Chapter Twenty-six

As soon as my plane landed at LAX, I let out a sigh of relief. I'd never been so happy to be stateside—America. However, my return home was bittersweet. I didn't have my gun, or my iPhone, which I left behind in Brazil. But I had my life, which felt strange now. I wondered if I'd ever be the same person I used to be. Even so, I felt a sense of happiness.

But my happiness wasn't long lived. I was met with two surprise visitors, Agent Jerry Stamper and Agent Richard Braggs aka Glass Eye, at LAX Delta terminal when I was trying to get my suitcase.

"So you made it," Agent Richard Braggs said rhetorically.

"What are you doing here?" I asked drily.

"We want that money," Stamper barked.

Their eyes darted back and forth between each other. I glared at them, my eyes filled with venom.

Almost like a movie reel being rewound, my mind went over a collage of images of what had happened since the Academy Awards a week ago. The image of Mayhem's battered face, the meeting with Tank, the getting Mayhem's boys safely out of town with Venita, the sight of Tank's beheaded face, the Santera in Brazil, the being raped, the almost being killed, then outrunning the anaconda until I shot it: it all flashed before my eyes. I'd seen too much.

I had been through too much to be afraid of either one of them now. I'd faced the devil and lived. They would have to bark up another tree. Now, my attitude was like, "Yeah, show me what you got." They were going to have to come with something stronger for me to be afraid this time around. I'd been to another world and back, and I'd really seen a cartel up close.

"I don't have it." My voice was flat, dead.

"We'll arrest you," Agent Braggs threatened.

"Then you won't get the money." I jutted out my chin with determination. I watched both men visually back up. I could see a dark cloud of evil surrounding both of these men. I wondered if this came from the magical amulet that the Santera gave me. It was as though I was on some higher consciousness.

"So you do have the money," Braggs said.

"Do you know where Mayhem is?" I ignored his question. My face was set in a stony expression.

"Do you have the money?"

"I'm not releasing anything until I get my brother." They didn't realize with all I'd been through, I was no longer the pawn in their game of chess. I was the queen and it was about to be checkmate time.

"All right. We know where your brother is. We'll make the call."

That's when I knew for certain that they were behind the kidnapping. I had to make a decision and I had to make it quickly.

"Where can we meet to make the exchange?" I asked.

"We're going to that Warehouse in San Pedro we took you to," Agent Braggs said.

"No." I was adamant. "Take me to the Venice Beach Pier. That's where I want my brother released. Out in the open. I know one thing. My brother better be alive." This was war. They were playing for keeps. Now I had to get into the trenches to do my guerilla warfare.

As we walked to their car, which was illegally parked in the drop off/pick up section at the airport, Braggs and Stamper gave each other a conspiratorial glance. Stamper nodded. After I climbed in the backseat of the unmarked government car, Agent Braggs stayed outside the car and made a phone call. I assumed he was calling the kidnappers, telling the where the drop-off point would be.

I chose Venice Beach Pier to make the exchange because I knew there would be crowds of people around as witnesses, and if they tried to take me or Mayhem down, hopefully someone would see it.

As we rode along in silence, I became suspicious. If Braggs and Stamper knew about the money, how did they know about the kidnapping? Wasn't that too much coincidence? What if they paid the Eses to do their dirty work? This way they got the money, and they broke off the Eses a little piece from it. What if this

was Mayhem's money? My gut started talking
to me. Something wasn't right here. I remembered what Tank said about how Mayhem had
gotten on the radar of bigger powers once he
started making more money. Investing money
on Wall Street.

I thought about how corruption wasn't just
something that took place in the hood. Corruption spiraled all the way up the ladder to
lieutenants, politicians, executives, judges,
bureaucracies, the government. Corruption is
everywhere. This was just high-level corruption in public service offices. Often jobs had to
be green-lighted from above.

Then it hit me. Who was to say this was their
marked money they gave to Mayhem? I'd already seen one of his miscellaneous accounts
and he had a billion in it. Three or four million
was not a lot of money to someone like Mayhem.

Moreover, who was to say if I gave them
the money, they would release Mayhem un-
harmed? My bet was they would kill both of us,
so I decided to change my tactic.

Agent Braggs climbed back in the car. Stamper
was riding shotgun. This time when the men
drove with me, they drove with care. They
weren't trying to drive like they were bats out
of hell now. No, they felt they were about to get
paid. I was no longer their mouse in cat paws. I
think they saw the look in my eye that said I was
not the one anymore.

It was almost noon, and traffic was heavy on
the 105 to the 405 North San Diego Freeway.

We were inching our way up to the Venice exit, so we could make it down to Venice Beach.

I thought about how Venice Beach might be a safe drop-off place. It was filled with shops, vendors, people. Yes, plenty of people would be there to hide behind. People would be out walking on the boardwalk, on the pier. There was the tennis court, people lifting weights, people handing out cards for doctors who prescribed marijuana, people eating at outside cafes. It was a long shot, but I had to think of a way where Mayhem and I might have a chance.

We finally made it to the dead end street you reach before you can walk to Venice Beach. We had to park on the street and it was about a five-minute walk to the beach to meet near then pier.

"Give me your gun," I ordered Stamper.

He turned around, looked at me, and hesitated.

"If you want this money, you better give me a piece. I know you have more than one on you."

Stamper looked at Glass Eye. He had a suspicious look but he also knew I was the one holding the money. That's when I knew for sure they were acting on their own accord. This was no covert government action. Agents, just like police, had teenagers to put through college, second wives to support, large subprime mortgages, just like the rest of people. Everyone was desperate and living on the edge. Desperate people would take desperate actions.

As we trudged toward the boardwalk, I looked off into the distance at the ocean. Generally, I would be happy to see the Pacific Ocean, but today, the ocean seemed dark, ominous.

Off in the distance, I saw someone push my brother out of a darkened van with dark windows, parked near the pier on the beach. Slowly, Mayhem began walking up the board-walk toward me. He still had that same proud regal walk. He held his head high. There were two men walking beside him, and from the looks of things, they were strapped.

I had just turned up the boardwalk, walking ahead of Braggs and Stamper, when, without warning, Romero appeared like a genie, pulled me to the side opening of one of the shops on the boardwalk. Once again, he had shown up from out of nowhere, just as he'd done when I first met him and he saved me from gang rape.

"What are you doing here?" I asked as he pulled me down.

As soon as Stamper and Glass Eye saw Romero's interference, they pulled their guns.

But Romero had the drop on them at the same time as he pulled his gun and held up his badge. "LAPD."

Immediately, I pulled my piece and, for a moment, we each stood, guns pulled, the two of us against the two of them, at a Mexican stand-off.

"Hey, this is a covert government operation," Glass Eye said, breaking the tension. "You're interfering with an operation we've worked on for months."

"Okay," Romero said. "I'm coming with Zipporah, though. Could you step aside for a minute? We'll be right out."

"You can't come with us," Agent Stamper protested.

"Okay, then. Let me just talk to this detective for a moment. This is a really dangerous move. You guys are putting her in harm's way."

"She'll be okay," Glass Eye snapped. A tic started under his good eye.

Romero whispered in my ear. "Z, be careful. They plan on shooting you and Mayhem once they get the money."

"How did you know?" I whispered back.

"I have eyes on the street. Why didn't you tell me you were trying to help your brother?"

"I didn't know if it was your family."

"It was, but they were just being paid to do the dirty work. These agents are dirty. They set up this whole kidnapping."

"I thought so. What can we do?"

"We're going to try to get your brother—"

Suddenly, in the near distance, I saw Mayhem haul off, cold cock one of his abductors, then break out running toward me.

"Mayhem?" I called out, interrupting Romero.

"Z, is that you?" Mayhem called out, flailing his arms about.

"Hurry up. Come in here," I said, running out toward him, blasting for all it was worth to try to cover my brother from the gunshots coming his way. Braggs and Stamper ducked behind another store.

Romero was close behind me on my heels. He was shooting his service revolver, trying to cover my back. A barrage of bullets flew out from all directions. I was just shooting back. At the same time, I was able to block Mayhem as he ducked down behind me. Ducking and covering Mayhem with my gun, I was able to get my brother into my hiding spot at the store.

The store owner, a Vietnamese lady, was shouting in a Vietnamese accent, "What's happening? What's going on? Don't shoot up my store!"

Meanwhile, people began stampeding up and down the beach, feet sounding like a herd of elephants. The young and old were hollering, screaming. Cries echoed all up and down the beach. "It's a sniper!"

"What's going on?"

"Run for your life! Duck!"

"Get Tae-Tae and 'em!"

Everything was happening so fast, I remember Romero running back into our little shelter. Mayhem had taken the gun out of my hand and was shooting back at his abductors.

Absently, I turned around to our hiding place. "Romero, where are you? I have Mayhem. What happened to those agents?"

I noticed that Romero was slumped over, leaned up against the wall. I don't know what I was thinking when I crawled over to where he was sitting. He seemed like he was all right, maybe just tired because he was bent over.

I took him in my arms. "Romero, are you all right?" I held his head back and noticed blood burbling from the corner of his lips. "What happened to you?" I screamed helplessly.

Suddenly I felt something wet.

I looked down and saw blood gushing from his chest. "Oh, no. Romero, you've been hit!" I began screaming and I almost blanked out, but I had to pull myself together. Everything seemed too crazy to fathom. How could this happen? Just when I decided I was ready to marry him. I held his head in my arms. "Hold on, baby. Hold on. I want to marry you."

Romero looked at me and tried to smile. "I'll always love you, Z." With that his head fell to the side. I touched his carotid artery. There was no pulse. Romero, the love of my life, was gone.

Mayhem had shot all his pursuers, or they had turned away. He turned to me, trying to calm me down, but you could hear my cries wailing up and down the beach, rivaling with the squawks of the pelicans circling over the ocean.

The two special agents, Richard Braggs, and Jerry Stamper, had disappeared like a mirage. I wondered if Romero had reported these two men to Internal Affairs. Did these two men want the American Dream so bad they would put their jobs on the line like that? I guess Mayhem was an easy target. He was dispensable for their plan. They figured they could get his money and it would be no problem. They didn't plan for Appolonia being held hostage with the money in Rio. They had probably planned to get the drugs and the money when she returned.

I thought of Mayhem. Appolonia. All of our fatal flaw was that we wanted the American Dream too. Later, I wondered, who were these two men? Were they just pretending to be DEA and FBI? Or were they were using the Eses to do their dirty work by paying them to do the kidnapping? They probably planned to keep the ransom money.

In this world, in Los Angeles, nothing is what it seems.

It was two weeks later, after Romero's funeral, that I realized I was pregnant.

Author Bio

Dr. Maxine Thompson is a novelist, poet, columnist, short story writer, book reviewer, book blogger, an editor, a ghostwriter, an Internet Radio Show Host for past 10 years, and a Literary Agent. She is the author of novels, *The Ebony Tree, Hostage of Lies,* and *L.A. Blues* and *L.A. Blues II,* Short story Collection, *"A Place Called Home"* (Kindle Bestseller), (Non-fiction) *The Hush Hush Secrets of Writing Fiction That Sell, The Hush Hush Secrets of Making Money* as a writer, a contributor to bestselling anthologies *"Secret Lovers," "All in The Family,"* and *"Never Knew Love Like This Before,"* (Also a Kindle Bestseller), *Proverbs for the People, Saturday Morning* (Contributor, and Edited Anthology for Saturday Morning Literary Workshop. She was included in Heather Covington's book, Literary Divas; The Top 100+ Most Admired African American Women in Literature.

(www.amberbooks.com. Released April 2006)

Notes

Notes

Notes

ORDER FORM
URBAN BOOKS, LLC
78 E. Industry Ct
Deer Park, NY 11729

Name: (please print): _____

Address: _____

City/State: _____

Zip: _____

QTY	TITLES	PRICE

Shipping and handling-add $3.50 for 1st book, then $1.75 for each additional book.
Please send a check payable to:
Urban Books, LLC
Please allow 4-6 weeks for delivery

ORDER FORM
URBAN BOOKS, LLC
78 E. Industry Ct
Deer Park, NY 11729

Name: (please print):_____

Address: _____

City/State: _____

Zip: _____

QTY	TITLES	PRICE
	16 On The Block	$14.95
	A Girl From Flint	$14.95
	A Pimp's Life	$14.95
	Baltimore Chronicles	$14.95
	Baltimore Chronicles 2	$14.95
	Betrayal	$14.95
	Black Diamond	$14.95
	Black Diamond 2	$14.95
	Black Friday	$14.95
	Both Sides Of The Fence	$14.95
	Both Sides Of The Fence 2	$14.95
	California Connection	$14.95

Shipping and handling-add $3.50 for 1st book, then $1.75 for each additional book.
Please send a check payable to:
Urban Books, LLC
Please allow 4-6 weeks for delivery

ORDER FORM
URBAN BOOKS, LLC
78 E. Industry Ct
Deer Park, NY 11729

Name: (please print): _____

Address: _____

City/State: _____

Zip: _____

QTY	TITLES	PRICE
	California Connection 2	$14.95
	Cheesecake And Teardrops	$14.95
	Congratulations	$14.95
	Crazy In Love	$14.95
	Cyber Case	$14.95
	Denim Diaries	$14.95
	Diary Of A Mad First Lady	$14.95
	Diary Of A Stalker	$14.95
	Diary Of A Street Diva	$14.95
	Diary Of A Young Girl	$14.95
	Dirty Money	$14.95
	Dirty To The Grave	$14.95

Shipping and handling-add $3.50 for 1ˢᵗ book, then $1.75 for each additional book.
Please send a check payable to:
   Urban Books, LLC
Please allow 4-6 weeks for delivery

ORDER FORM
URBAN BOOKS, LLC
78 E. Industry Ct
Deer Park, NY 11729

Name: (please print): _____

Address: _____

City/State: _____

Zip: _____

QTY	TITLES	PRICE
	Gunz And Roses	$14.95
	Happily Ever Now	$14.95
	Hell Has No Fury	$14.95
	Hush	$14.95
	If It Isn't love	$14.95
	Kiss Kiss Bang Bang	$14.95
	Last Breath	$14.95
	Little Black Girl Lost	$14.95
	Little Black Girl Lost 2	$14.95
	Little Black Girl Lost 3	$14.95
	Little Black Girl Lost 4	$14.95
	Little Black Girl Lost 5	$14.95

Shipping and handling-add $3.50 for 1st book, then $1.75 for each additional book.

Please send a check payable to:

Urban Books, LLC

Please allow 4-6 weeks for delivery

ORDER FORM
URBAN BOOKS, LLC
78 E. Industry Ct
Deer Park, NY 11729

Name: (please print): _____

Address: _____

City/State: _____

Zip: _____

QTY	TITLES	PRICE
	Loving Dasia	$14.95
	Material Girl	$14.95
	Moth To A Flame	$14.95
	Mr. High Maintenance	$14.95
	My Little Secret	$14.95
	Naughty	$14.95
	Naughty 2	$14.95
	Naughty 3	$14.95
	Queen Bee	$14.95
	Say It Ain't So	$14.95
	Snapped	$14.95
	Snow White	$14.95

Shipping and handling-add $3.50 for 1st book, then $1.75 for each additional book.
Please send a check payable to:
Urban Books, LLC
Please allow 4-6 weeks for delivery